Strange Dreams

Max Henninger

Orbis Tertius Press

Alberta, Canada

ISBN: 978-1-7781566-9-4

Table of Contents

Caracole

He hauled open the heavy old hulk of a door. There was no way of doing so other than slowly and the act unfailingly created an eerie sense of temporal dilation. Like a film sequence shot at less than the usual twenty-four frames per second. Entries into Syndikat were thereby lent a dramatic quality regardless of the entrant's appearance or behaviour. Enough to momentarily command the attention of each customer no matter how many beers deep.

But dilation was only the prelude to compression. This always reminded him of the student's convenient synopsis of Bergson. To understand time all you need do is imagine its converse. Everything happening at once. He was welcomed by a staggering simultaneity of impressions. Voices straining over eighties punk played at hard volume. The barroom's peculiar weather system of beer and liquor and smoke and perspiration. Humid intermundium pocketed away at the edge of Neukölln. Also the somewhat glassy eyes of Andi who was finishing what had been intended as a final tequila. He thought he detected a note of reproach in his voice. You can't be serious.

I am. Don't like it, go home. Flee as a bird to your mountain.

Andi surrendered and had one more. Minus the fruit. They raised elbows and shot the breeze for half an hour. Music and women. The usual. Eventually Andi got up and nodded goodnight with that grandfatherly mien he always assumed when tight.

Don't do anything I wouldn't do.

Already am. Signalling to the barkeep for a double scotch.

And forget about that Spanish lady. You don't have to pry all of them away from their boyfriends. It's not a contest.

Night, Andi.

They'd been over this already. Value of friendship. Importance of gratitude. Et fucking cetera. All very well yet no good. Being friends with Catrina seemed to him like a sun that fails to warm or Bushmills without the whiskey.

Night.

The door swung shut. He straightened himself on the bar stool and looked up at the fan spinning under the nicotinestained ceiling. Then he looked at the bottles above the backbar. Two rows deep though the mirror made it four.

Campari and Aperol and Ricard and Pernod and Martini and Averna.

Why had he never noticed that rubberlight draped over the dusty mirror? A hundred little bulbs like peas in a pod. Except the peas were embers. The pod a serpent's gut. And all of it so infernally serial.

Hennessy and Cuate and Habanero and Bacardi and Teelings and Hampstead.

Someone ordered coffee. The barkeep banged grounds into a wooden drawer.

Beefeater and Gordon's and Tanqueray and Herradura and El Jimador and Guerrero and Veterano.

Here was blackclad Oli now. Longhaired in a well groomed way and always the dictionary definition of levelgazed. Even at this hour.

Hello, Oli.

Hello. Where do I know you from again?

This place.

Aren't you a friend of John's?

Don't know anyone called John.

Oli blinked.

You don't know John? I thought you were a friend of his.

They seemed to have had this conversation before.

Well, said Oli. I'm going home.

Night.

Night.

Oli left. The door swung shut.

He sat and smoked. His reflection smoked back from behind bottlerows. Gargoyle in cinnabar light.

Maker's Mark and Four Roses.

He was resisting recollection's rearward pull. Steady like the suck of an outgoing tide. Fiery sundown tide. Lake of fire. Sea of fire. Hungry flames clawing oxygen from needful lungs.

Tullamore Dew and Laphroaig.

Water. Fire. Firewater.

Did he want to resist?

Yes.

Jameson and Glenlivet.

No.

Yes –

Glenfiddich –

and no.

Not really, no.

To hell with it.

He'd taken a long time getting ready for his date. Whore's bath over crusted enamel. Combing and multiple recombing. Threefold toothscrub with that petite lilac children's brush bought by mistake while in a hurry and used once by none other than her. There was something wrong with his molars. They were always aching. Especially at midday. This being to him what morning is to others. It was not the local ache of a spot of caries but rather a diffuse soreness caused by nightly gnashing of teeth. The associated nightmares woke him often. Moreover his gums had recently taken to bleeding profusely. Roseate foam circling the semiclogged drain.

The anguish exercising him during those few and ever encroached upon hours slotted for repose had not failed to mark his features. He often wondered how a face could look both puffy and tubercularly drawn. The puffiness was not that of the bored overeater but an expression of bodily decline. Perhaps of disease. He was going to the dogs. Rack and ruin.

He'd known he couldn't realistically expect to make as good an impression as he'd somehow managed on previous occasions. The reasons were obvious. Too little sleep and too much drink for too many weeks. After a month of sobriety he'd hit the bottle alone again. Half a quart of spirits on some days. He'd been ducking under the wave. This was the name he gave his preferred hangover prevention strategy. After drinking until dawn he would fall asleep with the lights on and then wake abruptly when his insulin rebounded some four or five hours later. He would get up and fix himself some coffee and begin his day before the headache could set in properly. The method had initially struck him as clever. Now that he'd employed it daily for weeks he was forced to admit certain flaws. Enough even to add up to utter ineffectiveness. His little trick amounted only to exchanging the occasional for the permanent hangover. With chronic sleep deprivation thrown in as a questionable bonus. Not to mention the eradication of anything resembling tranquility or focus.

Though the worst part was the sadness of knowing he was not only chiselling away at his own health and hope of happiness but undermining the tranquility of others also. He was perversely bestowing upon the world the very last thing it needed. Its nth quantum of misery.

You may still think of this in terms of sacrifice, he sometimes imagined himself telling Catrina. The truth is you're a smarter woman than you know for hitting the brakes before becoming acquainted with this man in earnest.

So it was wrath poured upon the desolate and snares rained on the wicked. But something else too. That the spell of alcohol can sometimes be benign, he'd told Andi during some previous session of theirs, is an observation whose verity is often acknowledged though its full import will eternally escape the understanding of the man who has never tried absinthe.

That so.

Yes.

You sure.

Damnation be my lot.

Absinthe.

Comes before absolute in the dictionary.

Ha ha.

Imagine a switch flicked inside your skull. All things suddenly illuminated by a light that is crisp and warm. Then again, no. It's not really an electrical affair. Not so much sixty watts as sixty candles. Yes, that's getting there. Sixty candles magically lit at the same time. Very soothing. And very exhilarating.

You're crazy. I'm going home.

Poverty and shame.

What?

Shall be to him that refuseth instruction.

Fuck you.

Fuck you too.

Ha ha.

None of wormwood's spell tonight. He was keeping the herbal fairy Artemisia absinthium snugly coiled in her bottle and sticking to rusty old scotch. Just fine for washing down those three beers he'd had with the Spanish lady. As Andi had called her. On an evening made of awkwardness and impossibility as well as occasional premonitions of death. Though mostly and less dramatically of undecidedness.

It had begun with the simple question of whether to have dinner straight away or drinks first. They'd opted for dinner at a venue suggested by her but then failed to find the place. Off to Al Andalos, she'd sighed after several inconclusive tours round the block. Al Andalos was a Lebanese diner on Sonnenallee. Alley of the Sun. An unusually poetic name for a city with more than a few thoroughfares named after perpetrators of colonial war crimes. Though in local parlance Sonnenallee was the Gaza Strip. A reference to its plethora of dime stores catering to the neighbourhood's Arab diaspora. Like a man baptised Maximilian or the Greatest but known only as Max. A name for dogs.

He remembered hoping Al Andalos wasn't the place he'd been to with Sara the other night. It wasn't. But it was being refurbished. The owner had stood between gypsum bags and waved to them through the locked glass door and mouthed the words: We reopen next week. So they'd decided that was that and started out with drinks after all.

Outdoor table on a less than level sidewalk. The ashtray and their beers had threatened constantly to slide down slanted firwood and shatter on poorly set cobbles. Not altogether conducive to relaxation but such were Weichselstrasse's bars.

Got a gift for you.

Her bigeyed surprise had made him want to lean across the table and hug her and he had. A near disaster for their lagers.

She'd fingered the soft cloth.

The last time they'd spent an evening in the park she'd brought a tin case of tortillas and a thermos flask of gazpacho but no blanket. Grass blades would have been their bed had he not spread his jacket on the ground. So she needed a blanket. Of course his gift was also a way of saying he wouldn't mind her taking him to the park again. Besides he'd known her long enough to notice a fondness for handcrafted objects and in particular handwoven textiles. There was a further and less obvious significance to his gift. He'd bought the blanket during a visit to Rabat and Rabat was a city whose residents spent half the night in cafés but didn't booze. He'd been on the wagon his entire stay and found it as easy as anything. A simple matter of doing as the Romans do. Andi's prediction he would make up for his sobriety once back in Berlin had proven depressingly accurate but Rabat remained to him a symbol of the man he could be if ever he succeeded in banishing alcohol from his life. Catrina had said to him she thought he could do it and should. The blanket was also a way of thanking her for those words.

If anything detracted from the satisfaction he felt over his gift it was this last aspect. He would have happily kicked the habit for Catrina's sake. But she'd made it clear this was to be their final date.

There had been an edginess to her. He would realize later that she'd been wrestling down her affection for him. She really had been on the verge of falling in love. This explained much of her inability to hold his eye or sit still. Though the immediate cause of her nervosity had been Reuben sipping a tall glass of hefeweizen two declining tables to the side. Reuben and Catrina's boyfriend almost certainly attended the same assemblies and protests. They might even have been friends. Catrina clearly didn't want Reuben to see them. Of course he already had.

Rosycheeked Reuben. Picture of good health. His was probably the only drink to lend those largely fatuous claims about beer's nutritional benefits some vestige of plausibility. German wheat beer was the sort of beverage even the World Health Organization might be moved to consider a meal. And a wholesome one at that. Reuben could easily have served as illustration. He'd known such people before and had even once come close to joining their ranks. People to whom life presented itself in athletic terms. As some sort of tournament. No problems and certainly no disasters. Only challenges. This couldn't of course be true. But if anyone looked the part it was Reuben. Barrel-chested and fairhaired. You never knew whether to admire or despise him.

He'd gone inside to pay for their drinks. When he'd come back out he'd rapped his knuckles on the rosycheeked athlete's table and nodded hello. Then he'd made his way past a brightly lit office space and a grocer's melon crates. Catrina had been waiting on the corner. She'd stood halfway inside a streetlamp's cone of light and this and her tense stance had for a moment lent her the appearance of some Weimar starlet.

He'd hugged her again. One hand on her shoulder and one on the curve of her lower back. Joyous flash in those dark brown eyes. The charm of that slightly bucktoothed smile. They'd paced from block to block in the direction of that Spanish place on the canal with her always a few feet ahead and him trying to roll a cigarette but more importantly to keep up.

This Spanish place had been her proposed solution to the dinner problem and it had gotten him more and more worried the closer they'd drawn to it. He really had been there before. With Tatiana. Take thirty-six or thereabouts of a key scene in the film of what was known as his life. Opens with a close-up of sunny infatuation before panning to gathering clouds of alienation and closing with a panoramic take of desperation pouring down. How was a man not to feel like the protagonist of some low budget production destined only for the dustiest of fleapits or more grandly but certainly no less unnervingly like the plaything of some bored extramundial stringpuller when faced with this blatant parallelism of locations and situations? This persistent recurrence? In fact no scriptwriter would have gotten away with it.

Por favor, respetemos a nuestros vecinos.

This had been taped to the door along with the menu of drinks and tapas. The place was called Gastón. Corner of Weichsel and Weser. Above the door flourished letters had spelt banally but also incontestably: La vida es breve.

He'd found the place pleasant enough in its conventional central European and early twenty-first century way. Young Spanish expats on the run from austerity. Toughfeatured and with the alert gaze of the stranger in town. Already hip to local fashion trends. Though he supposed those trends were not so local at all given the ever more networked character of personal computing. Full beard and tattoos in the style of Sailor Jerry for the barkeep. Bangs and bun for the waitress. He'd discussed such characters a great deal with Dorothea back when Dorothea had still spoken to him. This had reminded him of the postcard in his jacket pocket. The one he'd meant to drop in the mailbox on his way to meeting Catrina. Please call. Must talk. He'd forgotten somehow but resolved to take care of it later.

They'd left the tables to visibly well salaried wine drinkers and settled behind the bar. He'd watched and listened as she'd chatted with the waitress and ordered Spanish beer and the cheese plate and patatas bravas with aioli. I'll get this, he'd said. You can pay next time. Knowing of course there would be no next time.

Catrina had asked about Rabat. He'd told her about the cobalt blue sky and the souk and the cemetery. The cemetery is always on top.

The cemetery is always on top?

On the hill. Overlooks the casbah and the sea.

Their food had arrived. He'd lauded the salty cheese and she'd promised to bring some back from her next family visit. Then and with only mild resistance to his hand on her knee she'd launched into an account of the Spanish elections. The many young left voters abroad made the absentee vote decisive to the success of the socialists and the conservatives were doing all they could to obstruct. The elections are on Sunday, Catrina had explained. I'm a permanent resident and can vote at the embassy on Wednesday but temporary residents have to vote by mail. They need a form sent from Spain. Half the time it doesn't arrive.

He'd nodded wordlessly. They'd explored each other's eyes. He'd stroked her cheek and kissed her. As their lips had separated her gaze had strayed nervously sideward. His had followed and they'd found themselves contemplating a heavy black curtain drawn across a doorway at the far end of the room. It had looked to him like something from a magic show. Key prop from the disappearance act perhaps. But her associations had been funereal.

She'd moved out of his reach and recounted an episode from a book she'd been reading. About Madrid during the civil war. A wood shortage had constrained carpenters to fashion coffins from wardrobes. These had however themselves been in short supply and so many a coffin had lacked a lid. Paunches and noses of the dead had presented themselves daily to children peering from windows.

Tatiana had told a similar story in that very place. About Bosnian towns ringed with freshly dug graves. He'd stared hard at the curtain. Then he'd laughed in sudden comprehension of its mystery. The toilet, simply.

Catrina had begun to expand on the subject of children and he'd found himself more removed than ever. It always baffled him to hear such oddly general ruminations on whether a world of ever more gruesome bloodletting was one any woman could responsibly bear a child into. It never seemed to occur to any of the ladies expressing this concern that the health of the men they hoped to turn into fathers might be as much of a cause for worry. Certainly the first question he associated with children was whether he could reasonably expect to live long enough to see his wailing progeny shed its diapers.

Back on the street. Holding her waist and kissing her ear. What to do the rest of the night?

13

Take it easy, she'd suggested. Get some sleep.

Drink.

But not alone.

Final hug and caress. Final glimpse of flashing brown eyes and youthfully rounded jowl and energetically tendoned neck.

Catrina had headed to her apartment and he to Syndikat.

He watched the barkeep search for tobacco in the clutter of her narrow workspace. Basket of lemons and oranges. Chopping board. Beer mug filled with black straws. She looked good in her denim vest. Big friendly face. Slightly flushed. Straight blonde hair. The tobacco was in the vest pocket of course. She smiled when she found it. He smiled too.

Someone tapped his shoulder. The man at the table behind. Unkempt and more than one above the eight. A slow and clumsy roller.

Shower of beer mats. This was Conni in his light leather jacket. Ever squinting and grinning like the schoolboy who set fire to the chemistry lab. On his way to a game of pool in the back room. But not before telling the story of his recently quit job. Tending bar on Richardplatz. Wages two months overdue. And good riddance to the crossdistrict walk down Mittelweg and past the cemetery. Damn cold in December. Fresh fox prints every night.

More airborne beer mats. Conni seemed to be friends with the barkeep. At least they were tossing those mats as friends would. Which is to say they were mostly missing.

And now the blind man. A regular customer like himself though they'd never talked. Bumping into his shoulder and withdrawing with a mumbled apology. Feeling his way along the bar's scarred wood and to the next vacant stool. Balding giant. Thin beard. Benevolent and vaguely amused expression. Rough workmanlike features.

He ordered another scotch and thought as usual of women. Sara on top. Tying back her hair. Tatiana throwing him off balance. Redeyed Dorothea in the stairway. Catrina telling the story of her best friend. Three orgasms every time. Speeds their onset by crying out as loud as she can.

Catrina. Catrina. Catrina.

There'd been something of the caracole about their brief affair. Always turning but never all the way. She'd never strayed from that punctum indifferens beyond which the noncommittal ends. Not to tease him but out of some inner ambiguity abetted by his romantic fatalism. This fatalism was nothing he'd consciously elected but had long become habitual. A simple case of emotional exhaustion.

What should have been spontaneity had become some sort of kidney stone business. Obstructed and painful. Much as the liberating breath of air had withdrawn from the wide realm of physical experience to the narrow warren of phrases. Breathing had become for him a matter not of expansion and exhilaration but of their antitheses constriction and depression. The soreness stretched continually from his gullet to the lowest recesses of his lungs. Constant ache and burn. Should see a doctor maybe. Better not.

This complex of pain and apprehension couldn't but colour the entirety of his existence. It was hard to be carefree or entertain companions with anything other than sarcasm when haunted at all times by the consequences of his folly.

And what about those days his brain felt like it had been packed inside a shell of numbness while some weird spasm travelled his nervous system like the muted shudder of a subterranean engine? Oh no. Oh jactitations and asterixis. Oh fuck and was this to be the portion of his cup.

You must be the man the mason left that hole in the wall for.

He thought he recognized that voice.

What I told that son of a bitch. Skittering round like counterfeit money. Peddling hell knows what. Gives me a rash just thinking of him.

It was Robin. Short and stocky. Closely cropped peroxide blonde hair. Tough gunmetal eyes and mischievous mouth. Always talking louder than everyone else. She was in the company of a man with a shaven skull and a long black beard. Steady brown eyes under a Dostoyevskian arch of a brow. A blur of tattoos once black and now the pale green of oxidised copper spread up his neck and down his arms from under a baggy T-shirt.

He moved to the table and was welcomed with offers of rum and tequila. Robin introduced her companion as a visitor from the Basque country flown in for a friend's funeral. Robin had hosted the reception at her Kreuzberg beer garden. They conducted their conversation in a dockside medley of English and German and Basque and Spanish. The Basque was lost on him and the German on Robin's companion.

They compared tattoos. Spiders and bats. Born to loose. Stay true. Hold fast. Nobody knows the trouble I've seen.

Robin began talking about the dead man.

Real character. That time he climbed on the table and pulled off his shirt.

The Basque man nodded.

Fifties tats. Tiger across his back. All blown out. If he'd told me it was a zebra I wouldn't have known any different.

He bought la última and said goodnight.

Hermanstrasse was deserted except for two teenage shisha smokers slumped on folding chairs outside a late night store and a little man with a face grey as cardboard who asked him for a cigarette. No readyrolls but I've got tobacco and papers. The man took up the offer. He spaced the tobacco so poorly he had to gingerly unseal the paper and start over. Pausing once to fix a strand of ash blonde hair behind his ear.

You know Apo?

Don't think so.

Apo doesn't even try to be on time anymore.

Nodded farewell. He turned left by the water tower. A russet brick splendor in daytime. Castlelike. Crenellated even. Little more now than an overdimensioned mason jar looming blackly against the waning night. He descended Mittelweg whose sidewalk was a slalom trail lesioned by tree roots and wont to narrow and broaden for no apparent reason. Unless it was a matter of providing locals with space to discard mildewed mattresses and broken kitchen appliances. He rolled and lit a cigarette for himself. The flame surged blue and caramel from his zippo with a sound like wind hitting sailcloth.

Mittelweg. This had been Conni's way home. No snow this time of year though and hence no fox prints. He passed the cemetery and the little park that had once been a gravel quarry. Orion aslant above the beeches.

He crossed Karl-Marx-Strasse where the traffic light flashed amber and remembered to drop his postcard to Dorothea in the mailbox before steering himself on through Herrnhuter Weg's ammoniacal stench. Like a punch in the nose. He found his building and successfully battled the old nuisance of a lock by alternately slamming and gently rattling the poorly fitted key. He crossed the courtyard and climbed the two flights of stairs. Unsteady light from a naked bulb. Inside his apartment he headed to the bathroom and turned on the faucet and splashed cold water on his face. He turned the faucet off and stepped out of the bathroom and kicked the door shut behind him. He found his way to the bed. As he wrapped himself in the old sheets it seemed to him briefly that he had achieved a clear thought. But in the morning it was gone.

East From West

I. Meandering

Usted está aquí. You are here. He certainly was. In all the rumpled and malodorous glory bestowed by twenty-six hours of bad movies and worse food and turbulence and extended layovers. He rolled the cigarette he'd been jonesing for since Saõ Paulo and lit up. His eyes meandered from the metalframed map across a row of lampposts marking the perimeter of a parking lot and on to the faint dawn silhouetting a flagpole and the aerials and satellite dishes atop the flat roof of the terminal building. He drew on his cigarette and shook his head at an unlicensed taxi driver's offer. He eyed the enviably well rested security staff chatting and laughing to his side. A slim white arc hung low in the sky. The waning moon whose tips reached one way where Marco had come from but the other here. He smoked up and spat and lit his next and agreed eventually to another driver's offer.

Tenement fronts patched with corrugated iron. Bric-à-brac of jerrybuilt single-storey abodes nestled between public housing's concrete toes. Balconies fashioned from crate wood. A church spire behind rooftop water tanks. The words zona de niebla on a road sign.

The driver dropped him off on the as yet sleepy corner of

Viamonte and Suipacha in the microcentro. The fare had somehow increased by two hundred pesos. Marco only argued for a minute. He was new to the country and its language and told himself he could easily have come in for more thorough a fleecing.

It was several hours too early to ring Minina's doorbell. Tiempo Libre was the cafeteria he chose. Mainly for the ashtray on its single outdoor table. He deposited his suitcase under a window adorned with stylized palm trees. Un café con leche y dos medialunas, por favor. The owner was a man in his thirties with gentle eyes and a birthmark across one cheek. This seemed to confirm Marco's impression that he'd chosen a good place to sit and smoke and wait. Men in rubber boots hosed down the sidewalk. By Marco's third coffee it was about eight o'clock and the water had dried except for puddles under parked cars. The city came awake. Bells and horns and engines. Roller blinds were raised to reveal the display windows of bakeries and bookstores and kioscos. Curtains were parted behind balcony doors. Jack-hammers kicked into action to gnaw away at worn big city asphalt in their mechanical staccato. A cyclist swayed to balance the large bread crate on his bicycle rack.

Marco rang the bell at nine. He smoked another cigarette and rang again. There was a billboard across the street. A man in a mauve suit flashing a wolfish smile. The sort of character you wouldn't trust to spare you a match. Vivendas americanas. La casa de tus sueños.

Eventually Minina tossed him the keys from a first-floor window. She was in her early seventies. White hair cropped short above an alert and jocund face. She spoke only Spanish and this in a rapid chirp that reminded him somehow of the ridiculous lyrics of a song that had played during the overpriced taxi ride. She's a maniac on the phone and she dances like she's never danced before. Years later he would still recall Minina almost cheerfully announcing with remote control in hand that Francia está bombardeando Siria. But that was later.

He unpacked and ran through the old traveller's routine. A shave and a shit and a shower. He napped on the queensize bed that smelled faintly of detergent. By noon he was ready to explore the hosed streets. Like the tourist fool that he was he walked past Plaza San Martín and continued for several blocks more than most residents would have advised. He turned left behind Estación Retiro and passed the last stand selling ham sandwiches and found himself in a dusty unpaved thoroughfare traversing what he later learned was known as Villa Ocho Zero Uno. The place struck him as a densely inhabited agglomeration of construction sites. He snaked his way past cement mixers and piles of bricks and plywood and sought to comprehend the logic of this squatter settlement or slum. An embarrassing though perhaps predictable addition to the files of urban planners and the thirty-peso foldout map. Only a brief walk from the luxury apartments of Recoleta.

He found the absence of cross streets unsettling. Reminiscent of Lowry's Acapulco where the avenues of choice are few. No way to veer off sideways after thirty feet of wondering whether the man behind you has been thinking about how best to appropriate your billfold or is simply on his way to the dentist. There was in fact a dental practice. He saw the sign between a menu board and a refrigerator full of soda bottles.

Someone asked for a cigarette. A request Marco rarely refused. Here you go. Nice tats. Her name was Vanessa and she liked rock music. As confirmed by the Rolling Stones logo on her shoulder. By the time he walked on she'd given him her number. His departure was noted with relief by a cop who'd spent a good fifteen minutes standing a short distance away and doing his level best not to look like he was watching them carefully.

Marco returned to the legal part of town and noticed a photocopied flyer glued to various surfaces in rows vertical and horizontal. Another phone number and an image he took at first to depict a butterfly though on more careful inspection it turned out to be a close-up of some lady's buttocks. The image was rendered abstract by its relentless reiteration. A seriality disturbed only by the occasional doorjamb or drainpipe. Masajes 24 hs. Domicilios hoteles privados. He walked on. A headscarved spinster approached with outstretched hand. Que dios le bendiga, she whispered hoarsely upon receiving his small change. God bless you too.

Dinner on Lavalle consisted of a steak with fries and red wine. He tried to remember his conversation with Vanessa. Words spoken on a bench fashioned from two by fours and a pair of low sawhorses. Shaded by a gutted pickup truck. Only phrases came to mind. Mala via. Buena familia. He looked up from his fries at the street and saw a curlyhaired woman in her twenties pirouetting and shaking her hips at him and the other customers before hooking arms and turning the corner with a laughing middle-aged man. The female posterior, Marco observed, seems to be even more of an obsession here than elsewhere.

His thoughts turned to Marie and then to Anna and finally to Dorothea. Or rather he had a sudden vision of his hands on Dorothea's throat. Her eyes not afraid even then but charged with the blackest anger. He took a deep breath and counted silently to three. Then he returned his attention to the last of the fritas.

Terminó con la nariz rota en el hospital de Fernández. He terminated with the nose broken in the hospital of Fernández. This was the next morning in the airconditioned coffee joint next to Minina's. Marco sipped from his cup and was informed by television news of a salvaje ataque that had left some unfortunate young man assessing the merits of his city's medical facilities in un boliche de Palermo. Somewhere in the suburbs. Marco pulled a napkin from the chrome dispenser. The paper was waxed and oddly rigid like that used to wrap double-edged razors. He took another heavily sugared pastry from the plexiglass bell jar. Outside the jackhammers were at it again.

La cuenta, por favor.

A building on the far side of Plaza de Mayo prompted him to step outside the flow of pedestrians for a closer look. There were large black and white photographs on display to each side of the entrance. He found he'd come across one of those scattered though not altogether scant sites where the effort to erase history had been thwarted. Cortázar's fable. A city built on a cemetery. Here was a man in suit and tie with rivulets of black blood emerging from under his large glasses and here was a young woman walking with lowered head past a cordon of uniformed men. La noche de los bastones largos. Night of the big batons. Nineteen sixty-six. Not the end of the tale and not the grimmest of its episodes but then it seems that can always be said. Just a matter of how long you stay around.

More coffee on the corner of Perú and Belgrano. The place was called El Colonial. He struck up a conversation with the lady at the next table. She'd come to the city to have her computer fixed. Now she was waiting to meet her boyfriend and drive him out to La Plata. They were taking the week off. I used to always be in town Friday nights, she said. For the milonga. Was he planning to attend one during his stay? Marco shrugged and said he wasn't much of a dancer.

There used to be a place near the obelisco. I don't know if it's still in business. It was called La Ideal.

He remembered dance lessons with Dorothea and stinging shame. Once his clumsy execution of the contragiro or perhaps the sacada had sent his love to the floorboards and thoroughly blighted a day she'd looked forward to. The way he'd always seemed to steer them from joyful anticipation to disappointment and regret. At least toward the end.

La Ideal was still in business. He found it easily enough and looked at its chessboard floor through the window but didn't venture inside. Instead he rooted around San Telmo's antique shops. Broaches. A clasp knife with a brass handle. Dusty siphons and crystal flacons and heavy iron keys. Expert Watch Repairing. The dealers were eager to engage Marco in conversation. Where was he from, asked one upon hearing his broken Spanish. A tall man surrounded by alabaster lamps. Two or three questions and answers into their exchange they switched to English. Marco said something about how affable people seemed around here. The man nodded. We like strangers, he explained. It is because we are gentle.

Marco smiled. He felt he should make some polite remark about the lamps but nothing came to mind and so he cited jet lag and said goodbye. Less than a minute later he was jolted from idle musings by the sound of glass breaking. A bottle of Quilmes shattered on the curb of Nuevo de Julio. Two shirtless men were sizing each other up on the corner of a cobbled backstreet. One stood broadlegged in front of a squat darkskinned woman. Behind the woman was a child perhaps five years old. The other man snarled something incomprehensible. He was clutching what remained of the bottle. Marco walked on.

He passed bearded men lying under stained blankets alongside stashes of soda bottles and milk cartons. A heavily made up woman wearing pink panties over black leggings confirmed his observation about the female posterior by shaking her money maker at him all the way to the next traffic light. She addressed him in a gravelly whisper. Not very subtle though perhaps smubtle. To quote Aiken's Demarest. He shrugged apologetically. No entiendo español.

Everything around him seemed ostentatious. The streetlamps around a little park near the Kavanagh that were coming alight now one by one in a chaplet of electric flickers affected a grand belle époque style and were painted gold. The ombus would have been the pride of any arboretum. They struck him as the freakish product of some error of scale. Crowns the size of festival tents and roots tall as grown men. A family could with the aid of a ladder have picnicked comfortably atop any of those wizened grey tendrils. On Rojas a late night store brazenly boasted it was abierto 25 horas. Not to forget the police cars. A schoolboy's action movie fantasy. Fenders a foot deep front and back and more flashing and siren wailing than anyone could reasonably have claimed necessary. Seguridad, read bold white letters on the driver's side. Deber del estado, obra de todos.

The next day at nine he scooped the last of the milkfoam from his cup and brushed floorward a profusion of pastry crumbs while squinting at another television screen from the far end of that morning's woodpanelled corridor of a breakfast establishment. Panaderia La Madrid. Subtitles told the tale of Lucas and his recent consignment en manos de Dios by that showily vehicled policia metropolitana. The words slid by to the now familiar noise of jackhammers. El joven de 20 años recibió tres tiros. Uno en el cuello, otro en un testículo y el tercero en una pierna. Está muy grave. And nor would you, Marco told himself, feel so great after being shot in the balls.

Impudent close-up of the poor kid's mother at the site of the shooting. A generically suburban street corner shaded by plane trees. Mi hijo, las únicas armas que había, eran los sándwiches de milanesa que había ido a comprar para su familia. My son was armed only with veal cutlet sandwiches bought for the family. Marco wiped index and thumb on one of those rigid paper napkins and rolled the day's premier smoke and paid. It was pleasantly warm outside.

Every city has its colours, he mused, allowing ever cloudy Berlin as an exception. Here were greens ranging from dark bottle glass to bright swimming pool hues. Reds from oxblood to coral. A palette of blues including deep sea gloom and the flag's pale azure and another of yellows as varied. Among the more popular combinations were the blue and red of the colectivos and the blue and yellow team colours of the Boca Juniors.

The architecture struck him as a feast of juxtapositions. The ornamental married to the functional. By accident or perhaps to spite Adolf Loos. Parisian balconies and Roman stucco happily neighboured Londonian brownstone. Raw brutalist concrete and bland black steel dwelt demurely beside the lushness of heavily overgrown façades. Modernist metalwork and blistering paint. Mainly though the building fronts were those of the typical Latin metropolis. Lowered roller blinds and rashes of air conditioner fans. Wires dropping from rooftops to disappear under ledges or dangle lost above shifting traffic. Certainly this was what one saw the further one strayed from that thirteen lane gash crassly declared an avenue that cut from the edge of San Telmo down to Recoleta.

And then of course the sidewalks. When denied their share of attention they retaliated with bruises or worse. Potholes covered with splintering planks. Cobbles disappearing under a jetsam of plastic cups and fast food menus and candy wrappers. A jumble of urban detritus kicked about and trodden and pissed on by night and by day. The city's tirelessly renewed proof of habitation.

A paper streamer in the gutter reminded him of one of the better parties he'd been to back in Berlin. It had begun with him blowing just such a streamer at the laughing birthday girl. Beautiful Marie. Joy and ruin of his life. It had continued with plenty of beer and tequila and countless cigarettes and a lot of speed and molly. It had ended noon of the following day with Marie and Marco labouring to achieve orgasm on a red leather couch beneath a portrait of the young Elvis. Too bad about Marie. Not to mention Dorothea.

He got his hair trimmed in a little mouse hole of a barber shop. A poorly lit souterrain affair tucked away between a maxikiosco and a used book store.

Poco más aquí. Bien.

There were polaroids of a woman and two small boys stuck to the tarnished mirror. A pair of stainless steel thinning shears and a shavette with white celluloid scales lay on a leather mat beside an assortment of soaps and creams and waxes. Seventy-five pesos and a good job too.

Muchas gracias. Chau.

Suerte.

Newly groomed Marco walked north on Belgrano and was overtaken by a spring storm that soaked him badly and ruined his only pair of espadrillas. The storm began with a violet streak stretching scarlike across an abruptly darkened sky. The wind built rapidly and whipped leaves inside his collar. Little husks, he thought,

> blown with restless violence
> round the pendent world.

He quickened his pace as those goldpainted street lamps flickered alight to counter the gloom. Paper and cardboard items discarded on the street dissolved into a brown sludge. He found shelter under a ledge on Moreno. Somewhere in the thousands and not far from the Congreso. He stood contemplating the kiosco lights reflected in the flooded gutter and the ripples produced by impacting raindrops. Concentric. Like the Elizabethan world picture. Or Dante's hell.

He was standing on a generously dimensioned marble doorstep. Just shy of it was a small plaque that had been lowered into the sidewalk. Aquí fue coordinado tortura y detención. He looked up and discovered it was the entrance to the departamento de policia that was sheltering him. He had begun to pencil the plaque's full text on the back of the foldout map he was carrying when a uniformed lady with peroxide blonde hair tied back in a ponytail stepped through the sliding glass door to ask what he was doing. He'd already learned what to say in such situations.

No entiendo español.

The officer asked a great many questions whose meaning genuinely escaped him. Then she declared simply: Está prohibido. It is prohibited.

What exactly, he asked, and why?

Porque está prohibido.

Some people are difficult to talk to in any language, Marco decided. His pencil wasn't writing properly anyhow and the map was coming apart.

The next day was one for dress shoes. His espadrillas smelled like something awful and were consigned to the can. He managed to buy a new pair eventually and learned to call them not espadrillas but alpargatas. First he continued his studies of the microcentro's tertiary sector by getting his shoes shined on Riconquista. He settled into a metal folding chair and placed one foot on a slightly angled platform attached to the lid of an oakwood chest with dovetailed corners. The chest had a vaguely altarlike appearance and the objects deposited on it brought to mind devotional items. A tin mug full of steaming tea. A pair of cheap reading glasses. An assortment of small brushes grouped according to the colour of the polish they'd been used with. An indio in a tracksuit removed the lace from Marco's shoe and stuck a strip of heavily stained leather under the tongue and another in the heel. He proceeded to remove European dirt and dust using a regular shoe brush on the leather surfaces and what appeared to be an old children's toothbrush along the welt. He had one rag for applying an oily cream and another for shining and a large horsehair brush for buffing. When he was done he threaded the lace deftly back through the eyelets and began work on the other shoe. The entire operation lasted about fifteen minutes. It cost Marco thirty-five pesos and kept his footwear presentable for a good two months.

He discovered another plaque. Red clay framed by blue and orange tiles at 1730 Piedras in Comune 4 on the edge of San Telmo. Aquí vivo Elisabeth Kasemann, militante popular detenida, desaparecida el 8-3-77 y asesinada el 23-4-77 por el terrorismo de estado. No olvidamos. No perdonamos. Barrios x Memoria y Justicia. He thought again of Cortázar but also of Lowell. In a city of murder, an American city. Lowell had of course been referring to the Estados

Unidos. América del Norte.

He was on his way to La Boca. Mainly in tribute to poor old Paul Zech whose Michael M. irrt durch Buenos Aires he'd brought along from Berlin. La Boca was strident barking and the rumble of delivery van doors sliding open and shut. A radio playing behind a persienne painted blue and yellow in honour of the Juniors. Someone hammering in a backyard. A house on Suarez took the celebration of colour a bit far. The ground floor was mint green and the door crimson. The curtains in the window were olive and the upper floor was a sunfaded pink with a balcony also mint green. The buildings here were smaller. On a human scale. They looked mostly to have been built by their inhabitants. Corrugated iron house fronts. Firwood planks across steel girders.

Marco found the old ferry bridge. A smaller version of Marseille's transbordeur. Triumph of modernist engineering destroyed by Wehrmacht dynamite one shameful day in forty-three. He walked along the silty grey Riachuelo and saw fistsized lumps of nondescript vegetable matter float beside crumpled tinfoil. Three turtles swam slowly around a stick planted in the riverbed. One dove away and left a trail of lazily ascending bubbles. The water on the far bank was clear enough to mirror the red lattice boom cranes rising into the gunmetal sky.

Almirante Brown was a long and a poor street. Dime stores. Auto shops. Sometimes a bakery. Walls layered with weatherbeaten bills and notices. Fiesta en el barrio. Sáb. 7/11 19 hs. Shows en vivo. Tangos fatales. Entrada libre y gratuita.

Marco walked back to the city centre. He stopped by the Russian orthodox cathedral on Defensa. Five azure cupolas studded with golden stars and crowned with Saint Andrew's crosses. Familiar from Zech like the Lezama's plane trees and ombus that were still providing shade to old men and children as they must already have done during the luckless German's exile. He scaled the incline on the park's northeastern corner and paused before a frutería's pyramids of pineapples and oranges and bananas but in the end was drawn to the airconditioned ice cream shop next door. He waited his turn as three schoolchildren made up their minds and then was served generous scoops of dulche de leche and pistachio by an aproned man with a shiny skull and white eyebrows.

He returned to Minina's apartment via the San Telmo market and bought two ham sandwiches and a fifty centilitre bottle of red wine before shutting himself in the cool windowless space of his rented room for an early night. It occurred to him that in retreating this way he resembled his host. He'd seen very little of Minina since moving in. She seemed to spend most of the day and a good part of the night watching television in her own room. She didn't appear to eat or sleep or use the toilet very much. She was always in good spirits when they did meet. Cheerfully chatting away at him in her double-speed Spanish. He understood next to nought of what she said. What he managed to understand was that her late husband had played the bandonéon in a local orchestra and that she was voting for the conservative candidate Macri because it was time for change. Es tiempo de cambiar.

The next day brought more inclement weather. He stayed in his room to read. Every chapter or so he took a cigarette break on the cluttered balcony and listened to the revving engines of the colectivos and the horns of the radio taxis and the patter of the rain. Soft on the asphalt and more resonant on the awnings of cafés and fruterías.

By evening the sky had cleared and he went for a walk. He came across the aftermath of a protest rally on Plaza de Mayo. Macri posters had been torn from walls or defaced or covered with leaflets detailing the ever grinning businessman's rollback agenda and more particularly its antifeminist elements. A man in a stained jumpsuit was busy stomping flat discarded beer cans as others hosed away a mess of flyers and sandwich wrappers and orange rind.

Marco almost lost his bearings somewhere between Rivarola and Plaza Moreno. Bustle of homebound office workers. Neckties loosened at last. Umbrellas in hand. Occasionally someone stepped from the throng to climb into a parked car. When the taillights came on their red was reflected below. Winecoloured streaks in the last of the wet. He ended up in a little diner.

Rocca Resto-Bar

Bifé de chorizo c/ guarnición	$ 85		
Bifé de costilla c/ guarnición	$ 65		
Filet de merluza c/ guarnición	$ 65		
Pollo grillet c/ guarnición	$ 65		
Milanesa de ternera o suprema napolitana – fugazzeta o suiza c/ guarnición	$ 75		
Porción de fritas	$ 35	1 / 2	$ 25
Porción de puré	$ 35	1 / 2	$ 25
Ensalada mixta	$ 40	1 / 2	$ 30

Dirección: Bartolomé Mitre 1286

Reservas al: 4384-7014

Jueves, viernes y sábados de 18 hs a 2 am

A fan kept the flag on the far wall aflutter and shook the fronds of a potted cascade palm. Marco ordered a steak and a Quilmes and settled down at the smallest table. He studied the lettering on the glass door. It was backward from his perspective and read like something from a grimoire. 9971 yeL. ramuf odibihorP. The names of four of Doctor Dee's demonic familiars perhaps.

In the small hours Marco was smoking on Minina's balcony and noticed the office opposite was lit in a cruel electric glare. Windows stacked with ring binders and files. A grey man in a starched shirt defied union standards by typing steadily on a computer keyboard. Perhaps there was no union.

Marco looked down at the street where a lanky youth dressed only in green polyester shorts opened the front door to receive three visitors. Indios with bulging kit bags slung over their shoulders. If it was a drug delivery it was a big one. Probably just friends sleeping over. Later another young man rang the buzzer and waited in vain to be admitted also. He was too heavily dressed for the weather. Homeless perhaps. He paced back and forth for a good five minutes like he had some pressing matter to attend to before departing wildeyed and with a slightly spastic gait in the direction of the bus station. Later still the stocky middle-aged owner of a small kiosco stepped onto the sidewalk and lit up and took a long drag. He rolled his shoulders and withdrew the cigarette to blow ash from its cherry and then took another drag. Down to the filter in no time.

Everyone seemed restless somehow and Marco was no exception. When he finally settled into bed it was with nagging queries. What exactly was he doing in this city or for that matter this hemisphere? What the hell had he been thinking?

His body felt heavy against the mattress. He was tired. He told himself that in the end and no matter his motives or expectations it was near certain absolutely nada was going to happen. Yet something in his psyche's nether regions begged to differ as he discovered on waking some four hours later. He lay in the dark with dawn still a distant prospect and tried unsuccessfully to recall the details of his dream. There had established itself within him a strong sense of premonition. Something was gathering momentum and drawing nearer but remained for now beyond the horizon of his understanding. His capacity to define it.

The recommended eight hours had become an unlikely proposition. He thought of what Dorothea had written in her last letter. That like Freud's neurotics they'd seemed bent on transmuting pleasure into displeasure. That she wished he'd paused to think about his actions and that he'd seemed always to be in the thrall of some panic or desperation. That she wished she were less unhappy.

Marco lay on his side with his chest heaving and waited for the first sob to force its way from under his sternum. It never came and so he simply watched those familiar rosy fingers work their way under the door and edge back with reassuring persistence the shadows of wardrobe and desk and suitcase. Rhododáktylos Eos.

He got up in friendly sunlight and said good morning to Minina. She was outside her room for once to pass a purple feather duster over her bookshelves and she was singing something about fine weather. Another whore's bath and then breakfast on Lavalle. There was a story in the paper about the previous day's protest rally and the grievances that had occasioned it. Mainly the difficulty of bringing to justice the former dictatorship's internationally connected torturers and di-appearers. Basta de impunidad. Something else about the adolescent son of a policeman found shot in a suburban residence. There seemed to be a certain confusion as to whether he'd shot himself or been offed by his dad. One scenario was as plausible as the other. Some pages on Marco learned with schadenfreude that the former chancellor of his native federal republic, Helmut Schmidt, would next be seen in a wooden kimono. Ninety-seven years too many for the suicider in charge of Andreas Baader and Ulrike Meinhof and Jan-Carl Raspe, Marco thought. Whore of the liberal press and pretentious smoker of mentholated cigarettes. At least he didn't make the treble figure.

Never skip the cartoon. A woolyhaired little man noting the international observance of both the Día del Padre and the Día de la Madre and asking whether anyone has ever heard of a Dia del Edipo before concluding with raised hands that Freud's followers might benefit from some public relations work. Lo que le falta al psicoanálisis es el merchandising. For the second time in only a few hours Marco felt ready to cry. Not because the joke was so bad but because it made him think again of Dorothea to whom Freud's works were the Bible. His impulse was to tear out the cartoon and mail it to Berlin but he knew that was one impulse he wouldn't act on. Besides his synapses were demanding nicotine.

La cuenta, por favor.

An hour later Marco returned to San Telmo's antique shops and met César. A man he would remember among other reasons for his business card. Mercader de libros. Galería de anticuarios. Defensa 834. Above these words was a photomontage of el Ché and Gardel against a panoramic view of the city centre. The comandante was wearing his trademark beret and gazing upward and slightly sideways toward some distant socialist horizon. Gardel was wearing a creamcoloured fedora with a pinchfront crown and looking the other way. His eyebrows were slightly raised and his teeth showed in a half smile as if he'd just recognised some familiar face in the audience. Between this unlikely duo rose the obelisco's chalky phallus.

César was tasteful understatement in dress and neatly parted white hair and a trim beard. Short and a little on the soft side. The sort of man who eats well and uses skincare products. Bright eyes and a warm smile. Yellow teeth. There was a lascivious quality to his mouth. When amused by a remark he stuck the tip of his tongue out between his lips. César's stand was mainly books and records. Gardel on shellac. Cortázar and Borges in well preserved sixties pocketbook editions. An illustrated hardcover in the corner. Porque ser gay no es pecado.

They talked about translation and its impossibility. The Latin languages are a different beast from English, César claimed. English points you straight to the referent but Spanish and Portuguese and Italian create a space for the imagination to exercise itself in. Think of Dante's syntax in the commedia. A question of sonoridad. And that, the mercader insisted, was not just another word for musicality.

Cortázar's Rayuela became the subject somehow. A work that defies comparison, in César's verdict, except perhaps to Ulysses. Have you read Rayuela?

Twice. Once in English and once in Spanish.

And Ulysses?

Three times. Always in English. Though I'm sure it would also be a good read in your language. Especially that part about Bloom knowing how to deploy his tongue.

César giggled. Marco bought Ficciones by Borges in the 1956 Emecé edition and Las armas segretas and Bestiario by Cortázar in the 1965 and 1969 Editorial Sudamericana editions.

His thoughts that night were of none of those books. Nor did they return to Dorothea. Straddling the ledge of Minina's balcony with another fifty centilitres of red he pondered poor old Chet Baker splayed lifeless on the sidewalk before the Hotel Prins Hendrik. One short stoned plummet below room 210. Behold his hellish fall.

He survived his ledge straddling and even reencountered the marketer of books. But not before more café con leche and another day's paper. Marco had clearly been in town long enough to begin sinking into new habits. A pleasant moment to experience even when those habits prove later to be pernicious. He hadn't yet spent enough time to ascertain that. Also he was scheduled to depart soon. He would never graduate from the status of stranger. It felt reassuring.

Tourists are of course a pest, Marco continued his musings, though there's no denying that travel is generally both enjoyable and edifying. One learns. He was perhaps ready to sort through what he'd seen and arrive at tentative judgements. An angle of his mind had for the past few days busied itself establishing a typology of locally encountered women and was able by café con leche numero dos to present a first report. Prominent chin and full lips and assertive gaze. This was the type he gravitated toward most. Bangs seemed to be in fashion among them and to Marco's mind nothing was sexier than bangs. Also they didn't so much walk as strut and did what they could to show off their bodies. Undersized blouses and impossibly short skirts. This was all in contrast to the North American bottle blonde also often encountered in the neighbourhoods he'd been frequenting. Anorexic. Not so much stooped as cringing. As if expecting at any moment an infuriated father's blow to her nape. Those portable devices were presumably to blame. Dispositivos electrónicos, in his last flight attendant's diction. For a moment Marco thought he was perhaps just more redundant evidence that men are pigs. Then he thought for considerably longer about Marie and him fucking like duracell bunnies. His only compelling reason for returning to Berlin. As so often his poorly organised cogitations led to no conclusion. La cuenta and so on.

He needed to see that mercader again. During their last conversation César had said something about the difference between relato and cuento being lost in the frequent English translation of both terms as short story. This interested Marco.

César seemed glad to see him but said nothing of relatos and cuentos. He offered Marco a coffee and talked about himself. César wrote occasionally for a local paper. Articles on land reform and the boosting of peasant purchasing power through the creation of a robust domestic market. Marco sympathised though he also detected an undercurrent of poorly understood Marxism that irked him. He did not however articulate this. Another customer wanted to pay and Marco stepped outside as César attended to business. Some five minutes later they continued their conversation on the sidewalk. Marco noticed César used a cigarette holder. Lilac bakelite.

The mercader asked the usual questions. What did Marco do for a living? Was he married? Did he have children? Was he gay? Marco was economical with his replies. Brief silence. César noticed sulphurous stains on Marco's index and middle fingers and recommended investing in pumice stone and lemons. Pulpa de límon. Works wonders. Marco nodded absentmindedly and flicked his thumb against the back end of his rollup to release the ash that had built up on the cherry. He mentioned Macri's election campaign. The paper had informed him that one of the ministers in waiting was a Catholic zealot who considered homosexuality and contraception and pre-marital fornication so many of Satan's snares. Incompatible with the gospel and hence to be tirelessly combated by government. César was unimpressed. It's only the right, he said. La derecha. Those people always talk like that.

They finished smoking and said goodbye. Marco was about to leave when César looked him over and chuckled. What's this, César said, the tricoleur. Marco didn't understand at first. Then he glanced down at his clothes and saw what was meant. Red shirt and blue pants and white alpargatas. The colours were in the wrong order but close enough. Marco laughed.

Vive la France, the mercader called after him as he walked down Defensa.

II. Refraction

Marco had now been in town for seven days. His second and final week was a change from the first insofar as he spent the better part of it in company. This was of course both a blessing and a curse. Opening his eyes to some truths even as it blinded him to others. Minina had taken in a second lodger. His name was Eugenio but he was not Italian. He was French. In fact the first discovery Marco and Eugenio made about each other was that they were both sham Italians. My parents liked Montale, said Eugenio. Mine met in Liguria, said Marco. Little seaside town called Albissola. My mother took me back there most summers. I'm Markus by passport but my summer friends called me

Marco and it stuck. My summer friends were my best friends.

Eugenio had arrived from Chile. He hadn't seen his native France for some time. He was a physics teacher with a good knowledge of astronomy and had left his wife and daughter in Toulouse to work for half a year at the La Silla observatory in the Norte Chico. This had helped him get back on the wagon after a period of excessive drinking. Three bottles of white a day. He'd decided to travel back to la grande patrie via tango's international capital. He was giving himself five days to see as much of the city as he could. Eugenio was apasionado del tango. Marco wasn't sure he liked the man but was charmed by his toothy smile. Reminiscent of sunlight breaking through some North Atlantic pea soup of a sky.

During one of his recent perambulations Marco had come across a bar cum café formerly patronised by the bandonéon player Anibal Troilo. El gordo Pichuco, as he was known locally. Eugenio expressed interest in seeing the place. They went and had coffee. Marco would have liked to drink his corretto. With a shot of grappa. He would have liked to order whiskey as that had been el gordo's preferred libation. But he did neither of those things. Nor did he tell Eugenio about how the efforts of Pichuco's wife to keep the dressing room free of liquor only led to the obese virtuoso arranging for someone to pass him a flask from the wings.

The place was called La esquiña de Anibal Troilo. A short uphill walk from Minina's on Paraguay. Burgundy awning. Tall windows. Chessboard floor of worn marble. The walls were covered with photographs and paintings of the famous patron. Also newspaper clippings and other memorabilia. A certificate above the bar declared the establishment a café notable. A sunfaded clipping explained that el gordo Pichuco iba ahí todos los días cuando el café ostentaba estilo bohemio y se llamaba Del Carmen. Dicen que siempre se sentaba en la misma mesa y que tomaba whisky. Above Marco's and Eugenio's table hung the facsimile of a membership card issued by the Club Atletico River Plate. Number 885. Funny, Marco thought. El gordo seemed to him to belong with the Bocas and not with CARP. Now owned by none other than that moneyed dirtbag Macri.

Eugenio didn't know much about the bandonéon. Weird kind of

accordion? Don't say that to a bandonéonista, Marco replied. He'll tell you it's more like a piano. Bellows and buttons notwithstanding. A Schifferklavier, as we say in Germany. Sailor's piano. Invented in the eighteen forties. Commissioned according to some by a congregation that couldn't afford an organ. Named after its inventor Heinrich Band the way the saxophone is named after your countryman Adolphe Sax. Same era roughly. The bandonéon predates the accordion by half a century or so and was eclipsed by it because the accordion is easier to play. Though some people including yours truly would say the bandonéon sounds a hell of a lot better. No one knows what it is but everyone's heard it. Think Piazzolla. Your tango music wouldn't be much to write home about without the fueche. As they call it here. Means bellows. Argentina is where the instrument came into its own thanks to late nineteenth-century German emigration and the musical inventiveness of this town's immigrant community. Legend has it some German sailors ran out of cash at the bar and paid the tab by leaving their squeezeboxes. The things were built by a handful of family businesses near what is now the border between Germany and the Czech Republic. Mining region broken by British competition circa eighteen eighty. Unemployment breeds emigration and so a lot of these instruments travelled overseas and ended up here around the time Italian and Caribbean and local indio rhythms coalesced into what eventually and inscrutably got called tango. Inscrutably because no one knows where that word came from or what it means exactly. While everyone knows what jazz means or at least used to. Something you wouldn't say in front of a lady. Anyway. Piazzolla the maestro harvested the fruits of tango half a century after it all began. Having cut his teeth performing with Troilo. Then there's a fellow called Mosalini who befriended Cortázar during their shared Parisian exile. Not to forget Binelli. Wrote a piece called París desde aquí. From Paris to here.

Marco's monologue seemed to be losing focus. He mentioned Rayuela. Moves between Paris and here too. Have you read it? Eugenio shook his head. Marco began to talk about the role French military advisors had played in the Argentine dictatorship's crackdown on the opposition and more specifically the junta's torture methods.

Electrically charged batons came straight from colonial Algeria. Sort of a westward transfer of anticommunist technology.

He sensed he was losing Eugenio and swung back to the subject of tango. Albeit not very elegantly. Just another middle class fad these days if you ask me. Wasn't always that way. When tango hit big in your capital back in the twenties the Argentine ambassador was alarmed. Beseeched the ladies not to go to those dances. Brothel music. They were doing their share of cocaína in the orchestras. The lyrics of the older pieces make rap look like nursery rhymes. All about knifing people. And pussy. Seem to remember a tune called Dos sin sacar.

Eugenio chuckled uncomfortably. Marco felt he should check his mouth. Been to La Ideal? Place by the obelisco? Eugenio hadn't but La Ideal was closed. No matter. The astronomer had looked up a dance class in San Telmo and was in a hurry to get there. They parted.

Marco went for a walk through Montolivet before returning downhill to the microcentro's congested bedlam. He noticed a waste container that seemed to have become the object of some desperate ransack. The dome lid had been swung arear and there was nothing inside except a can and a yogurt cup but all around were straining trash bags stuffed with tins and vegetable trimmings and coffee grounds and the odd condom. Mounds of refuse rose from the street like sea wrack from a beach. As if someone had climbed inside the container and tossed out everything he didn't require before leaving with the rest. Marco couldn't make sense of it. He wasn't to see his first cartonero until after his date with Natalya.

He napped at Minina's and had a salad in one of the diners on Florída and strolled about some more. He had coffee in a sunless cramped little café and watched the couple three tables down sulk over a beer and a lemonade. The man was resting his face on his hands and leaning forward slightly towards the woman. She was leaning back and looking away to the side. She was very thin and her knees were trembling. The man began speaking and she covered her face in her hands. This seemed to make him speak faster and more animatedly. When he'd finished she lowered her hands and looked at him calmly. Es pesado, she said. Insufrible. Es tiempo de cambiar. The man began speaking again and spoke at length but the woman seemed hardly to be listening now. She was looking away to the side once more and interjecting the occasional si or no for appearance's sake. Marco signalled to the waiter. Señor. Por favor. La cuenta.

He walked around Recoleta for a few hours. Past brightly lit boutiques and shops selling silverplated calabazas and other Creole handicrafts. Sundown found him in a café and bar on the corner of Chacabuco and Juan Roca. White marble floor. Walls painted a dark mustard shade above the wainscoting. At the next table an obese indio stared dully at a bottle of Coca Cola and a shot glass brimful of bourbon. A large mirror facing the window reflected conversing pedestrians and a businessman stabbing with one finger at the touchscreen of his mobile phone. Motorcycles and cars and buses rushed past behind them. Above hung the darkening sky. Streaked with mauve. Marco found a newspaper he hadn't studied yet. He read an article about an cfcctivo de la policía bonaerense shooting his girlfriend and then himself. Another on the rape of a young woman in a Caballito driveway. El ataque ocurrió en la madrugada del miércoles, cuando la chica regresaba de un local de comidas rápidas.

He rejoined Eugenio for dinner in one of the restaurants featuring what was known as the tango show. This consisted of a heavyset man with a black beard and unkempt hair playing the bandonéon rather listlessly. He sat hunched over his instrument and walked his large fingers over the worn galalith buttons with their mother of pearl inlays in such a way that each musical phrase was accompanied by a subdued mechanical clacking. Decades of playing had exposed the pearwood and spruce beneath the instrument's dark shellac finish and its nickel silver reinforcements and decorations had lost their lustre. The bellows paper was the traditional Gustav variety with its swirling marble pattern. Burgundy and gold.

No one aside from Eugenio and Marco seemed to be paying much attention to the music and Marco suspected the player of cutting short his set when he clapped the bellows shut a final time upon finishing a slow vals and swung the old box from his knee onto the floor and got to his feet and rolled up his sleeves and headed for the bar.

So now you know what a bandonéon is, Marco said. It's very

beautiful, replied Eugenio. Sort of groans and grumbles and wheezes but sings as well. Like a little orchestra with its own bass and its own violin. Though I'd say the player didn't exactly put his heart into it. Would you say he seemed a little bored? Marco shrugged and reached for a toothpick. Let's just hope his drink is on the house.

At two in the morning Marco was smoking on Minina's balcony and looking absentmindedly at the fluorescent lamp suspended by wires above Viamonte's still busy traffic. He noticed a spider had spun its gauzelike web from one wire to another and across the lamp's steel casing. The web bulged precariously when struck by wind gusts arriving from Nuevo de Julio but it held and Marco returned indoors with a feeling of reassurance. He browsed the old lady's bookshelf and found a Spanish Bible and opened it to the Book of Psalms. Como está de lejos el oriente del occidente, así alejó de nosotros nuestras transgresiones.

His dream that night was of Paris and of his father. Slain recently by sudden cardiac arrest. Marco's parents had divorced not long after his birth and his childhood and adolescence had been largely father-less. His genitor had spent four decades lecturing on Robert Musil at Nanterre. Marco had spent a week living with him in the quartier latin and had suffered daylong treks from one library or museum to another. He remembered the travel more than the stations. The ache in his ankles. His eyes directed mostly at cobblestones and sometimes at film posters intimating obscure worlds of violence and sexual trespass. His dream restored to him the tedium of those wanderings in a vision of bus stops and flourished bottle green metro signs and narrow sidewalks that was uncanny mainly for the profound sense of direction accompanying it. A feeling he wasn't simply meandering but bound for a chosen place. Though he had not been the one to choose it and had no clear notion of it. No way of naming it. As if his feet knew where they were going but his mind did not.

He woke sweating and drythroated to Eugenio rummaging about next door. They met in the hallway with toothbrushes in hand. Eugenio said the tango class he'd meant to attend that day had been cancelled. Marco mentioned the Gardel museum and before he knew whether he wanted them to be they were on their way.

Eugenio was delighted to learn their host country's national hero had been born in France and what's more in Toulouse. El mago, as the critics had dubbed him. Cardboard panels narrated the ever smiling baritone's brief sojourn among the living. From emigration to aviation and the tragedy of that Colombian plane crash. They inspected Gardel's fin de siècle furniture and various other items including his guitar and a rather battered bandonéon. Didn't know our magician played the fueche, Marco commented, then thought he probably didn't. The instrument's inclusion in the exhibition struck him as a result simply of the curator's antique shop connections. Yet there the tired old squeezebox was. The second they'd encountered in two days. The dark goatskin gussets spread open as its bellows lay fully extended across the display case like the nude splayed across a bed on some erotic daguerreotype. On the oblique corners of the wooden lids was the traditional nickel silver intarsia. A three-stringed lyre Marco liked to think of as stretching from disaster to remedy and from transgression to pardon.

Outside the museum was a construction site. Eugenio was studying newly purchased postcards when he nearly stepped into a pit that dropped a good six feet below the sidewalk. Marco grabbed his arm in time but then both of them almost fell in the path of a furiously honking colectivo. So much, thought Marco, for disasters and their remedies.

He spent the afternoon in Parque Lezama. Resting and smoking in the shady nook between two ombu roots. Four teenage girls were playing frisbee under the Russian cathedral's azure cupolas. Later he slalomed through crowds of norteamericano tourists to the San Telmo market hall. He had a sandwich and a cup of coffee and read the paper. A feature story told of several hundred squatters turning the political limbo of this final pre-electoral week to their advantage by seizing fifty hectares of land on the edge of a suburb called Merlo. Almost though not quite like the preferred red of bachelors the world over. Local highrise residents were not pleased. They'd taken to shouting insults and hurling vegetable projectiles from the colectivo whenever it took them past the settlement. Las familias de Merlo no se van y crecen las tomas en la provincia.

He had dinner with Eugenio at a buffet restaurant near Plaza San Martín. Bright canister lighting. Greasy stainless steel steam tables. Checkered oilcloth. They shot the breeze over ice water and an assortment of legumes neither of them could have cooked more blandly even during his student days. Eugenio spoke about scientific discovery and its injustices. Take refraction, he said. Light waves change direction as they move from one medium to another. Descartes is widely credited with elaborating the first satisfactory theory of this phenomenon. In fact a fellow named Snell or Willebrord Snellius developed more or less the same theory at pretty much the same time and most people have never heard of him. But it gets worse. A certain Thomas Harriot had it all figured out about twenty years before Snell. Thirty-five before Descartes. There was also a gentleman by the name of Pierre de Fermat who got his head around the problem by working from something called the principle of least time. People say this shows discoveries are in the air. Waiting to be made at certain historical moments. As decreed by the Weltgeist, I suppose. Most of those people don't know about Ibn Sahl of Baghdad. He solved refraction's riddle a good half millennium before the others. Seems to me one could be forgiven for wondering just how many of our discoveries are really rediscoveries. Do the all too evident limits of our ability to communicate and cooperate condemn us to work out the same problems over and over? Marco chuckled. Science as Sisyphean endeavour. Ewige Wiederkunft des Gleichen. Shall we go for a walk?

They did after Eugenio and the cashier had resolved a disagreement over the question of second helpings. There was shouting. Then dolares changed hands and everyone agreed to be nice.

During their walk Eugenio began to speak about Alexander Graham Bell. The man who upon graduating from Edinburgh University had invented the telephone and was not to be confused with Graham E. Bell, the contemporary yanqui astronomer and discoverer of close to a hundred asteroids. Alexander Graham was merrily experimenting with undulating electrical currents and their correspondence with sound waves and suchlike until in eighteen seventy-six he filed a patent application for the popular dispositivo that keeps so many of us in touch with our mothers. The application nearly fell through because an engineer from Ohio by the name of Elisha Gray had struck on much the same idea at roughly the same time. So who got there first? We argue over it to this day, Eugenio said, meaning by the plural pronoun that international commonwealth of scholars on which Marco was often glad to have turned his back. Though that seemed like nineteenth-century history too.

Colectivo. Policia. Traffic light. Marco rolled and lit a cigarette. Jackhammers stuttered angrily. In the shadow of a doorway across the street a money changer called out what seemed the entirety of his vocabulary. Cambio. Cambio.

The next day Marco didn't see much of Eugenio. Each minded his own business as if they'd overspoken or exchanged too many confidences.

The second day after their dinner of legumes catastrophe called. It was viernes, 13 de noviembre. There was an article in the paper on why thirteen is considered an unlucky number. Judas the thirteenth man at the table. Though it was the television and not the paper that confirmed the old superstition. Marco was in the panaderia having a late morning coffee when the dusty screen informed him that ninety rock fans had been gunned down by members of a Middle Eastern militia with aspirations to statehood. This had transpired in a Paris theatre and nightclub named the Bataclan after Offenbach's operetta. Marco's rock days were largely over but he could imagine a slightly younger iteration of himself at the gig. One that would now perhaps be in a body bag while his remaining friends and relatives struggled to reconcile the unexpected turn of events with their naïve but hardly uncommon assumption of a world in which most things turn out alright. Or with a little more luck he would be alive but considering trauma therapy. Marco found it difficult to accept such truths himself. The more simply and starkly they presented themselves the more they seemed to belong not to the realm of the real but to one more properly characterized as subreal. Apologies to André Breton.

He paid his tab and smoked a cigarette on the sidewalk. Then he went upstairs and knocked on Eugenio's door. The travelling astronomer was still in boxers and wifebeater. He was sitting on the edge of the unmade bed and balancing a laptop on crossed legs. Marco leaned over his shoulder and joined him in perusing Le Monde's breaking news. Tales of sudden death and of its anguished expectation. Images of flowers and candles arranged before fractured windowpanes. La brutalité de l'attaque a laissé la communauté sous le choc. Le président a déclaré l'état d'exception.

This daesh or ISIS or ISIL or estado fucking islamico was really something else. Suicide bombings and crucifixions and decapitations. If this is what the revenge of the dispossessed looks like, Marco thought, count me out. Minimal standards of peaceful interaction asserted for decades by pallid diplomats seemed to have become the object of some fury of negation. Marco wouldn't have voted for those diplomats given the chance but he was willing to concede the decency of their intentions. Now everything seemed a matter of proving all the reactionary hogwash true. Clash of civilisations por esempio. Just how was history to proceed under such circumstances except by running along that well worn groove of hostility and retaliation? The sheer folly and futility of it. As if those of us not born with a golden spoon up their ass hadn't already been having a hard enough time just making it from one month to the next.

Later that day Minina swung open her bedroom door looking flustered. Francia está bombardeando Siria, she exclaimed. Le Monde confirmed the French republic was stepping up its antiterrorist Opération Chammal by striking targets in the town of Al-Raqqah. Tit for tat indeed. No doubt historians would later argue over who started.

Eugenio left the next morning. Marco helped carry the twenty kilos of luggage allowed by the aerolina to a radio taxi waiting on Nuevo de Julio and wished him a safe trip before stepping into the nearest maxikiosco for an early beer.

That night he lay in bed drunk and listened to the gale building outside. Rain against the balcony door. Pit pat. Pidda pat. Pa ridda pat. He thought of the Chet Baker plaque outside the Prins Hendrik. Of a paper streamer sailing in jubilant defiance of gravity across a barroom. Of Marie squinting in the sunlight reflected by a houseboat's double-pane window. He thought of Dorothea. Of her eyes aglow with injury and anger and of how much easier everything would have been if he could have dealt with those feelings consecutively. He knew it was unheard of. Double pain. Dorothea pleading with him in the stairway. These storms were what they were and the clemency of orderly proceedings was doomed to remain a fantasy. A particularly naïve one in fact. Ridda pa ridda pat. Somehow the roof was always blowing off.

III. Aftermath

Ginebra, the barkeep repeated softly, pouring him a shot. Marco took a small sip and understood. It was gin. He looked at the lawn green label. La llave. And by way of illustration: a key with an ornate bow and a fluted shank hovering magically above the national flag.

Is good, no?

Marco nodded.

Very good. Muy bueno.

Memories of the day. Natalya on the stone steps of the university. Slightly stooped and keeping her distance from the smokers and drinkers. In her eyes that had studied him discreetly by the evening light he'd detected a subdued apprehensiveness. They'd established by an hour's conversation and by walking from one end of San Telmo to the other and back that they could probably trust one another and so they'd settled down to an overpriced dinner and some white wine on that square by the market hall. Mostly international students at the other tables. Natalya hadn't been quite what he'd expected. Her big feet that he'd kept bumping against under the table. Her slightly overshot jaw and that shock of roughly cut black hair. A shy boy. Well, he ought to have known.

The day had begun with an article on domestic violence. A statement: that la casa es ocho veces más riesgosa que la calle. A tally: 277 asesinatos vinculados al hecho de ser mujer en 2014. Some warm words occasioned by the death of someone called Francisca Pesetti. Francisca quedará por siempre en el recuerdo de todos, por haber sido una de las mujeres más bellas que dio la tierra del sol y del buen vino.

He'd read another paper over lunch and come across an interview with a former Tupamaro recently released from prison. Fifteen years. Most in solitary. No visitors for three months. Then a private screening of a film made of the crackdown prompted by the first and last attempt to break him loose. He was allowed to walk the prison yard alone for fifteen minutes a day. Then for thirty and eventually for an hour. What did he do the rest of the day? Pace his cell throughout the morning and most of the afternoon just to be able to sleep at night. Of the revolutionary project that had led to this predicament he said it was justified then but unthinkable today. El mundo ha cambiado.

Later Marco had paid César another visit and talked about Zech. German writer I've been reading.

Zech?

Yes. Paul Zech.

César's lips had closed round his cigarette holder. Expressionist poet?

Marco had nodded.

I think there was a parallel edition published some years ago.

Zech is mainly remembered as a poet but also wrote prose. Travel books and short story collections and novels. Strange character. Rather the despair of his biographers. Liar and impostor. Much of the secondary literature still mentions his doctoral degree. Fact is he made that up. Like many widely reiterated claims about his background and employment history. He was also what you might call a reverse plagiarist. Published some moderately well known translations of Villon. Except they weren't translations at all but his own verse. Took scholars a few decades to call him on it. You could say meretriciousness was the secret centre of the man's life. He was married to two women at the same time. Spent a few weeks in Dottyville. To borrow Buck Mulligan's name for the psychiatric hospital. In thirty-three he lost his day job at a Berlin library when it was discovered he'd stolen upward of two thousand books. He was politically out of favour for having been involved in that Bavarian socialist experiment fourteen years earlier. Hitler's bureaucrats didn't forget such things. When it all came to a head Zech took a train to

Vienna and another from there to Trieste. Then the boat to Montevideo. Ended up in this town. Those travel books he wrote about his journeys through Brazil and Chile and Peru are utterly fraudulent. He was never in any of those countries. Though he did get to know the ciudad autonoma pretty well. Wrote seven novels here. Of which only one was published during his lifetime. Not the best. He was in poor health towards the end. Simply collapsed on his doorstep one morning in the spring of forty-six.

I don't like what you tell me about the library books, César had said. Though I'll be sure to look up his novels.

You should. That parallel edition. You wouldn't happen to remember the title? César had furrowed his brow. If you don't remember it doesn't matter.

I do remember. It was called Yo soy una vez Yo y una vez Tú. One time I'm me and one time I'm you. Pretty good title. But what did he mean?

Marco had looked at a mottled eggshell button dangling by a thin thread from César's shirt and at the ash sloughing from the cigarette in his holder. Then he'd looked into the mercader's friendly blue eyes. No idea. A liar's honest moment perhaps.

In the evening he'd gone to meet Natalya. Anna had given him her number. He'd put off dialling it out of a sense that meeting anyone who knew him or even just his last affair would falsify his experience of the city. An experience he wanted to be pure. Why after all does one travel? Though of course he'd known he would call her eventually. Two days before his return flight it had seemed alright.

You must have been flattered, Natalya had said upon hearing he'd spent the better part of a summer in bed with her former Berlin roommate. For the preceding decade or so Anna had preferred women.

Let's just say it seemed appropriate to the exceptional nature of the larger situation. We helped each other break up with our girlfriends before facing the fact we could never make a couple ourselves. Two-year relationship in Anna's case. Ten in mine. Quarter of my life. Will you have another?

They'd spent the rest of the evening discussing the subject of

Natalya's dissertation. Kant's theory of incongruent counterparts. Perfectly equal and similar yet not to be included within the same boundaries. Like snails whose shells twist opposite ways or screws of the same dimension but threaded in opposite directions or human hands completely alike except one is derecha and the other izquierda.

The evening had concluded with Natalya heading to the bus stop and Marco being introduced to the local gin. The next day he ventured forth from Minina's for his second and final date with the guarded boygirl. It was raining and the walk to the steak and fries restaurant where Natalya had suggested they meet proved longer than Marco had anticipated. He counted his money in the doorway of a department store and decided he could afford a taxi but arrived a quarter of an hour late all the same. Natalya was sitting at a table by the bleared window. He spoke a greeting and sat down across from her and removed his wet jacket and hung it on the back of the empty chair next to his and ordered a scotch.

They talked politics. Those squatters in Merlo were as sure to be evicted as Macri's electoral campaign was to prove a success, in Natalya's judgement. Macri is part of a larger trend, she said. The whole of South America is shifting to the right. The left will make a comeback but it will take them a decade or so. A cyclical affair. Most people aren't interested. Politics is a circus to them. They don't see its relevance to their lives.

After dinner they had coffee. Marco ordered more scotch. The conversation turned to Anna and from her to questions of romance. Natalya was curious about Marco's involvement with Anna and by implication Dorothea. Marco was beginning to feel slightly drunk but retained enough control over his faculties to present one of the shorter versions of the story.

I thought I would spend the rest of my life with Dorothea. She was the first comprehensively beautiful woman I met in Berlin and the reason I didn't leave after a year or two. But within half a decade our relationship turned into a cruel nightmare of disappointments and suspicions and recurrent accusations. Sometimes spoken but mostly unspoken. We had terrible fights and kept the neighbours awake with our crying and shouting and smashing of furniture. This was always followed by weeks of radio silence and then by slow reconciliation. But the next time was always worse than the last. So many dress rehearsals, it seems to me now. I met Anna translating for activists at a protest camp in rural east Germany. You could say she was my ticket out. Though what really ended the drama was a trip to Amsterdam with Marie. One of Dorothea's closest friends. We went to a show at the Paradiso and visited the Prins Hendrik on the way and took pictures of room 210 whose windowsill Chet Baker fell from. Hero of mine. It's not important. We also smoked too much dope and before long the terrible union was consummated. As the bard says. I'd been unfaithful for years. Lying and cheating like my life depended on it. Maybe it did. But this was in another league. Dorothea wrecked my apartment when she found out. When I dragged her into the stairway she rang every doorbell she could reach and told my neighbours I'd tried to strangle her. I told her I never wanted to speak to her again. She left. The next day I packed her things in a bag and hung it on her doorknob and threw in my key to her apartment. I changed the lock on my door. Dorothea spent two weeks in psychiatric treatment. Your former roommate decided this was a good moment to propose redefining our affair as what she called a serious relationship. I told her no and drank all day for a month. Then I called Marie. We've been seeing each other since. And fighting some too. When we're not fighting we drink together and do a lot of speed and bone the nights and mornings and early afternoons away. She'll be waiting for me at the airport if I have any luck left in this world.

Natalya had moved herself as far back into her chair and the chair as far back against the one behind as possible. She sipped from her glass of water and studied Marco silently for a long time. When she spoke again she used the expression folie à deux. Marco was now more than half seas over and heard himself laugh loudly.

Excuse me. He coughed and lit a poorly rolled cigarette. He placed the cigarette in the yellow tin ashtray on the table and removed a thread of tobacco from his underlip. Then he picked up the cigarette and drew on it at length. Dorothea was fond of psychoanalytic theory and I've read some of those books myself. Not sure it helped me understand anything much though such reading does provide one with labels to pin on behaviour repeatedly observed in oneself and others. Projective identification for example. Means you'd like to strangle someone but find yourself unable to do so and settle for telling his neighbours he tried to strangle you. The first thing you learn concerning folie à deux is that it's never à deux. The Oedipal triangle asserts itself without fail and so every relationship goes not two but three ways. The third player is typically some parental phantasm. Though this theory of triangulation is also invoked to explain infidelity. Which is where it goes wrong as far as I can see. Let's say Dorothea brings in her father and I bring in my mother but also Anna and then Marie. Surely each of them brings in a few more people. So what you end up with is not a triangle but a manypointed star. And that has always reminded me of Malcolm Lowry's favorite misspelling of the word disaster: disastar. Marco's cigarette had gone out. He relit it and concluded. They'll make a thousand explanations but disastars will continue.

This prompted a hint of a smile from Natalya. Marco felt in good form and resumed his monologue. The problem is we lose room for manœuvre the longer we play these games. You bleed and then you reconcile and then you bleed again. It's been called a wearisome tide. With the completion of each cycle another part of you perishes. There comes a point at which your options are much reduced and that saving stir of love and fellowship proves definitively beyond reach.

Natalya asked for a cigarette. He pulled one of his acacia gum papers from the booklet and smoothened the paper's edges with thumb and forefinger. He cupped the paper and strewed tobacco inside and spread the tobacco uniformly from end to end. Then he rolled and sealed the cigarette and handed it to Natalya and lit it for her. She nodded thanks.

The problem is loss, Marco said, and the way we are hopelessly overtasked both by our experience of loss and by its anticipation. The problem is fear. Fear of facing the absence of what has gone as well as the transience of what is here now but will certainly forsake us at some unknown point on time's forward trajectory. All of us and especially those of us most attached to life are familiar with the fantasy of jumping onto the tracks as the train pulls in. Which is to say of destroying what we cherish most. The world given only by virtue of our existence. This always reminds me of my father whom I loved unreservedly. I've found that postmortem talk of his indisputable qualities is liable to stimulate some perverse and childish part of my mind to formulate insults. I love you, loved you, therefore fuck you. What is it that makes us lash out at those we need most? I think I know. It's fear. The possibility of some lethal accident becomes less terrifying once you imagine the accident not as an accident but as something you have willed. Once you imagine yourself as the event's author. Some atavistic psychological mechanism turns the prospect or memory of losing another's love almost into a source of pleasure as soon as you envision the loss as issuing from your own action. This is perhaps why we do all we can to sever our bond with those we depend on. We sense our togetherness must end someday. One way or another. So let us at least be the ones to snap those scissors and drop that bastard of a curtain.

Natalya drew on her cigarette and stubbed it out. She sipped again from her water glass.

Once you start down that road it's hard to stop. Someone called it the law of series. You know the German proverb. Ein Unglück kommt selten allein. It's banal and brutally true. Misfortune seldom presents itself in the singular. Loss after loss. One horror opens into another. And of course the worst and most haunting misfortunes are the ones we bring upon ourselves. Have you read Hudson? Tales of the Pampas? Piece in there called El Ombú. To one who has lived long, Marco recited, there is not one spot of ground, overgrown with grass and weeds that is not equally sad. For this sadness is in us, in a memory of other days which follows us into all places. Old as the hills. Juvenal speaks of the punishment of not being acquitted by the verdict of one's own heart. Oddly enough what this leads to is not despair or at least not what most people associate with that word. What it leads to is freedom. Something like omnipotence even. Though there too the common associations are misleading. The omnipotence I mean is founded on nihilism. A confidence of success that is utterly hollow because it will never lead to satisfaction. I can achieve anything, says the man possessed by this feeling, because nothing has meaning any longer. What had meaning is what I have lost.

Natalya stifled a yawn. Marco wanted to order more scotch but didn't. He rolled another cigarette for himself and lit it. What you're left with, he said, is mainly the need to recalibrate. Everything is familiar yet also foreign. As in Freud's definition of the uncanny. Everything is changed. The elements remain in place for the most part but are governed by some new logic.

It was time to call it a night. They stood up. Marco almost knocked over the table and realised he was drunker than he'd thought. He managed somehow to accompany Natalya to the bus stop and say goodbye and promise to be in touch. He even memorised her directions to the nearest taxi stand. They struck him as both complicated and vague. Of course he never found the taxi stand or rather stumbled right past it. Up the hill to Nuevo de Julio and on toward the microcentro and Minina's. He asked himself more than once during this journey of an hour and a half what the hell he'd been saying and told himself it didn't matter. It was only so much verbal spindrift above the rolling ocean of his confusion.

The rain hadn't stopped all night and began to beat down harder now. Marco found himself pondering the concert or more accurately the cacophony of his fears. Fear of folding in on himself like a house of cards. Of losing his will to do anything at all. Fear of falling short once too often and being finally abandoned. Fear of the undirected anger that was the outward counterpart of his sadness and would at times strike out randomly like a heavy iron part flying off some madly locomotive machine. Wantonly destructive. Fear of the undefined but terrible penance he often felt was coming to him. Fear of finding one day he'd lost all his friends and betrayed all his loves and failed at most every endeavour and that his life was for all purposes over. Though he could of course continue going through the motions and try his best not to burden others by sharing the realisation. Quietly mourning what he'd allowed to slip by or cast away until some slight but ruinous mutation triggered the colonising action of cancer cells in his lungs or his gall bladder or his blood. He felt despair pressing fiercely down on his sternum. Always these anxieties. Could there ever be relief and if so what would it consist in? He remembered

Minina's Bible. Como está de lejos. As far as the east is from the west, so far has he removed from us our transgressions. The words made him smile though he sensed immediately they would never be much help. He remembered Aiken. Where is the east hemisphere and where is the western. Do you use narcotics.

Fear of terrorist attack didn't feature somehow in his catalogue of disastars. Fear of grave injury and disfigurement did. Fear of assault and of physical cruelty. Fear of guns and knives. Mainly of guns. Fear of castration and blindness. Fear of soldiers and policemen. Fear of disease. As during the summer when each deep breath had prompted a stabbing pain behind his twelfth rib or those mornings some undiagnosed internal hemorrhage had turned his sputum roseate. Fear of being unable to breathe. As when he'd fallen from a wall onto his frail teenager's back one distant afternoon. Standing up to stare bewildered at the other boys and find his lungs stalled. Or during that harsh Manhattan winter a decade later when a week of ample drink and reckless chainsmoking and no sleep had brought on a bout of pneumonia. He'd sat in bed all night because to lie down had been to drown agonisingly. Incapable of drawing more than the slightest breath of air. Utterly terrified by the corset some malignant spirit had placed around his thorax. Fear of public failure and mockery and contempt. Fear of losing Marie's love and the attention of the other sex more generally. Or even interest in the other sex as seemed to befall some men with age. Fear of seeing his cherished voluntary solitude transformed into the much less appealing involuntary variety. Fear of lasting ostracism. Fear of failing to impress. Fear of disappointing those he admired or whose affection he treasured. Fear of disappointing sexually. Also fear of invoices and bank statements and tax assessment notices. Fear of the coupling of insecurity and aggression often encountered in young men. Fear of ignorance and folly. Fear of depths and heights and vast open spaces and deceitful seas.

He pictured Marie at the airport terminal. The intelligent benevolence of her gaze and the way she was capable of smiling with her entire body.

The rain was finally relenting. A waxing gibbous moon showed through the clouds alongside a scattering of the brighter stars. He thought of Blanqui's Éternité par les astres and wished he'd quoted it to Natalya who was now presumably riding that colectivo or resting in her unknown bed. Tous les corps sont reliés l'un à l'autre par les choses mêmes qui les séparent.

Hours later he would be haling his own twenty-kilo luggage allowance streetward with the stairs of Minina's building cascading above him like bellowfolds. But for the time being it was vacant sidewalk after vacant sidewalk. Lights flashing at deserted crossings and reflected spanglelike by the sheets of water below. Then a single stooped cartonero dragging his cart one block ahead and straining wasted muscles to plod stoically up the next incline.

Strange Dreams

I. Circles

Lisboa. Walking in circles. Mostly uphill. Round a scaffolded corner and past debris of renovation. Up heroically proportioned escadinhas. Steps for giants. Far too high and less than level. A trial for Marco's quadragenarian knees and lungs. Hats off to the local pensioners. Like that bent spinster behind him on Madalena. How did they manage? He crossed a small square paved with white cobblestones. Largo de some saint or other. A single tree in the far corner. Four oranges in a nest of bottle green foliage. More plodding ascent of escadinhas. City of seven hills. Such fun. Marco's suitcase seemed to be getting heavier. He was wheezing and sweating. Walking uphill. In fucking circles.

He didn't want to call the city a labyrinth. That term was tainted. Marie had used it to describe a certain Berlin night club. Never mind the name. Some memories hurt more than others. How much better it was to recall that miserable little dog on the subway. A scabbed and stunted creature perched precariously on an accordion player's shoulder. It could have passed as an ugly cat. A paper cup in its teeth. Three copper coins inside. Marco had made it four between Cabo Ruivo and Olivais. And then the blind man with his telescoping plastic cane. Hard to tell whether he was simulating. The dog had begun to yelp frantically upon catching sight of a poodle sheltered between a dourfaced passenger's knees and the accordionist had almost botched his trite tune on his way to the steel door that had clanked open then at Chelas.

Marie had looked like death when he'd met her for coffee at the edge of the park. Know where I've been?

I know.

He supposed he would have looked pretty pasty himself after that much coke and a night in that fucking hell hole. Though of course he was only jealous and would never have thought of calling it that if she'd taken him along. Well. How exactly did he expect her to take him along when the main reason she'd gone was Annabelle? Whose white lace panties he'd been in the process of pulling down past those pretty knees around about the time Marie had been smiling her way past the bouncers. And just how many more times did they need to live through such episodes before something in their now painfully familiar relational setup repositioned itself and cleared a little space for even the vaguest intimation of a new experience?

He remembered the band-aid on Marie's left index finger. She'd cut herself cooking dinner for Julian.

It was as usual complicated. And he'd finally reached the hill-crest. Rua de Achada number eight. A narrow building of two floors painted a pale rose colour and overlooking another cobbled square. This one had a slight slope to it and there was a little iron stump of a water fountain at the lower end.

He unpacked and showered and then he walked around some more. The Castelho loomed first to his left and then to his right. The sky darkened. His knees ached. He was hungry and began to look for a place to have dinner. Santo André seemed like it would do. A restaurante and cervejaria with white plastic tables under a green awning. Showcase of fish by the door. Salmon and cod and sardines on their bed of ice. Concentric grey and eggshell pattern of the mosaic tile floor littered with empty sugar packets and the plastic film torn from a cigarette pack. No credit card, read a black vinyl sign. Não há serviço de mesas.

He sat down at one of the tables to study the laminated menu. On the back of the menu was a soft drink ad. White swirl lettering on red. He put the menu down and looked around to take in more of his surroundings. By the door was a morning glory in a terracotta pot. A second refrigerated display case held little glass bowls of mousse au chocolat and some sort of vanilla dessert. A soccer match played silently on a flatscreen television. On the countertop was an old Faema 61 espresso machine. Next to the espresso machine was a wooden statuette of the Virgin Mary in a goldpainted robe. On the wall was a soccer scarf in the national colours. Porto campeão do Euro. Two shelves of liquor and one of herbal tea and another of potato chips in aluminum foil bags. The sound of people talking quietly at indoor tables blended with the clink of cutlery on plates. From the kitchen came the hiss and sizzle of some fried dish.

Marco ordered a glass of vinho verde and the bife de atum. The latter arrived on an earthenware plate. King of the seas swimming not in the briny deep now but in golden olive oil. Alongside three boiled potatoes and a sprig of parsley. The sort of meal Marco had hoped for.

A man in black slacks and a black wool sweater sat alone at one of the indoor tables. He was in his late sixties. Age spots around the edges of a closely trimmed beard. A rascally glint in soft brown eyes. His smile revealed widely spaced teeth stained a weak grey. Marco was finishing an espresso when the man stood up with one hand on the small of his back and a little grunt of discomfort. He shuffled into a dimly lit backroom from which came the sound of people stirring. Someone spoke a few words that Marco didn't understand. Then chords were struck on a guitar. A second guitar joined the first and a serious guttural voice launched into song. The delivery was half spoken to begin with but soon took flight in an energetic crescendo. Marco stood up to see. It was the old man singing. He stood broadlegged in the centre of the room with his hands on his hips. Behind him sat the two guitar players. Both were about his age and dressed in worn black suits.

Marco listened for a while and decided to look into this fado business. Then he paid and left. Annabelle had recommended a bar on the western edge of Graça. El Botequím. He found it easily enough and stayed for several drinks but concluded it was not a serious bar. There was a shelf of paperback novels and travel guides on one wall as seen sometimes in youth hostels. The old wooden ladderback chairs and the ceiling's yellowed stucco had a certain charm but this was spoiled by the gaudy emerald wallpaper with its flourished gold patterning. The barkeep was in her twenties and served his second and third orders with a look of disapproval. Marco's drinking was perhaps not in keeping with the World Health Organization's advice but why this should have irked her escaped him given that he was sober enough. The difference between a good barkeep and a bad one, he thought, is the difference between judicious and judgmental.

He got up early the next morning. It was Sunday but he found an open pharmacy that sold him some cotton wool. A Moroccan convenience store owner indifferent to the Catholic calendar sold him a wick and some flints and a small can of lighter fluid. He took his purchases back to the apartment and set about repairing his zippo. It had been gutted by an overzealous German at airport security. He threaded the wick through the eyelet and folded the tip of the wick to prevent it from slipping back out. Then he tore the cotton wool into little lumps and packed them into the inner case in lieu of the usual rayon balls. He soaked the cotton with fluid and secured the felt pad. He removed the flint spring and dropped a flint inside the tube. Next he reinserted the flint spring and tightened the screw. Finally he set the wick upright and tested the cam and slid the inner into the lower case. When he struck the flint wheel the flame leapt blue and gold from the perforated chimney.

Marco often ran into trouble at airports and train stations. He supposed his contempt for the uniformed was to blame. Though to be sure it had been a plainclothes cop who'd taken him to the precinct and strip searched him once as punishment for disregarding the smoking ban at Munich central. Or more likely for telling the bastard to piss off.

How long his trip from Berlin had seemed. He recalled the protracted layover at Brussels airport where he'd sat slumped on an uncomfortable steel bench listening to monotonously delivered announcements. Please make your way to gate sixty-three. We are now closing the gate. He supposed some passed the time by perusing Pessoa or the Financial Times. But he hadn't been able.

On Monday he bought trinkets for friends. A pair of brass and agate earrings. A bottle of port wine. Some sardine tins with colourfully illustrated labels. An old wall tile with a maroon and olive floral motif and another with a white arabesque on an ultramarine background. Lavishly tangled lineation. He stepped inside a store selling wool products and flirted with the saleswoman for a quarter of an hour. She was hoping to visit Berlin that summer and keen on pointers. It was only while talking to Gus later in the day that Marco realised what had drawn him to the store. A coat in the window identical to the one Annabelle had worn on their first date.

So how do you know Annabelle? Gus asked when they met downtown for any early dinner and drinks.

We met at the Akademie der Künste. The Academy of Arts. She was pitching a theatre project to sponsors.

She lives in Berlin now?

Only until the summer. For the duration of the project.

You're part of this production?

Marco smiled and shook his head.

One of the sponsors?

Marco chuckled.

I was the interpreter. What I do for a living. Translation and interpretation.

Gus also sometimes took on translation jobs though he had to be careful because he wasn't allowed to work in Portugal under the Schengen treaty. Much of the evening's conversation revolved around the inconveniences the treaty's numerous and often obscure stipulations created for an Israeli citizen such as him. Gus was hoping to secure a second passport for himself on the basis of his family's Polish background.

Marco wasn't impressed by Gus' choice of restaurant. It wasn't a restaurant properly speaking but a cultural centre run by a cultural association set up by some young people with an interest in music and theatre. That was all very well but the food was terrible. There was also too much of it. Soy products were the main ingredients. A bland meal that tasted mainly of good intentions. Moreover Marco was expected to stand up from the table and step outside before lighting up. Each time he did so he incurred from Gus a look equal parts disapproval and condescension.

When they said goodbye outside the Anjos station around midnight their encounter almost concluded in openly vented hostility. Marco tossed his dog end on the curb and Gus launched into a harangue about littering that was so emphatic in its condemnation of the petty transgression Marco couldn't help wondering what larger imbalance lurked behind the outburst. He felt for a moment that a riposte was in order. My dear Gus, he almost said, I know you think I despise you for your sexual orientation but you're quite wrong. I might even have flirted if you'd been a little nicer. So I went to bed with your Lisbon roommate of long ago. What does it mean? Pick fights with all of her lovers and you won't get done in this life. Have you heard me complain about our vegan excuse for dinner? If you're so concerned over what I'm doing to my lungs and the sidewalks of the Portuguese capital perhaps you should move to California or for that matter Bhutan. Nationwide smoking ban. Would that be to your liking? Stop being such an aggrieved little dictator. I could be your friend.

Of course none of this was voiced. They simply went through the motions of a civil farewell as best they could. Marco spent half his subway ride penning an imaginary letter to his sometime Berlin bedmate that amounted to an extended interrogation on her approach to matchmaking and travel and life more generally.

In fairness the evening had not been without its moments. They'd spent a pleasant hour or so in the basement of a café where they'd watched a tall and rawboned Japanese man sit stooped on a stool and lose himself in a trance as his fingers picked adeptly along the neck and body of an acoustic guitar. A fine musician who had in all likelihood been classically schooled. Researching the city's free of charge musical performances was one of Gus' pastimes and his choices for the night proved his taste. Marco had burned through twice the daily budget by buying too many double scotches at the second venue they'd visited. A large bar with a balcony and a view of the city sloping down to the river. Three guitar players had strummed

Latin tunes to a cheeryfaced cachon player's rapid slapping of his seat cum instrument. Gus had sat in sober contemplation while Marco had eyed the blondes and jonesed for his next smoke.

Marco woke early the next morning. He showered and dressed and stepped outside. He pulled the old wooden door shut behind him by its heavy iron knocker and plodded up more unevenly spaced steps to a weedgrown alley that sloped upward and downward in the shade provided by whitewashed three-storey buildings with roofs of terracotta barrel tiles. He needed coffee and found it in a gloomy single-room establishment. Pastelaria Varanda. Four white plastic tables and a refrigerated display case with two tuna sandwiches inside. On the counter were a chrome napkin dispenser and an electric coffee mill and a stainless steel juice reamer. A sign advertised ice cream products with names like Solero and Fruta Fizz and Twister. Next to the sign hung an embroidered wall cloth displaying a stylised bowl and the words: Há sopa. On a small shelf were cigarette packs and a box of disposable lighters and another of lollipops. As well as three bottles. One of port wine and one of cheap blended whiskey and a third of something he didn't recognize.

Bom dia. Um café e um sumo de laranja.

Two women in their forties sat at one of the other tables. Grocery bags by their feet. They spoke mainly to each other but occasionally addressed a question or comment to the owner. A man with hornrimmed glasses and short white hair who was dressed in the manner of many of the city's elderly men. Grey slacks and a dark wool sweater with the collar and cuffs of a checkered shirt showing. He walked out from behind the counter to explain something. He traced lines in the air with one finger. Perhaps a map. The ladies nodded rapidly to signal comprehension and launched into an extended commentary whose meaning escaped Marco.

He had just finished his coffee and was rolling a cigarette when a greeting was heard from the doorway. A third woman stepped inside carrying her own grocery bags. She was obviously acquainted with the other two but much younger. There was something plaintive about her. As if she'd just become the object of some malicious remark or insult. She bought the two tuna sandwiches and stashed them in one of her bags with several paper napkins. When she left the older women resumed their conversation in which the owner participated occasionally as before.

The owner turned his back on his customers to polish the electric coffee mill with a small blue dishrag. He was saying something but the ladies ignored his words and drew their heads together in a hushed exchange. They stood up as if suddenly in a great hurry and picked up their grocery bags and stepped onto the street almost shouting their goodbyes.

Marco finished rolling his cigarette and paid. He had agreed to visit the local feira or flea market with Gus. Marco had a fondness for flea markets that was less a matter of the objects on sale than of the people those objects attracted. He'd mentioned this to Gus and Gus had told him he was in the process of furnishing a two-bedroom apartment his parents had recently purchased for him in one of the inner city's last affordable neighbourhoods. Gus was planning to live in one room and rent out the other. He wanted to decorate the apartment with old musical instruments. Guitars and violins and maybe a concertina.

All Gus found at the feira was a pair of badly battered flutes. He seemed pleased with them. Marco bought more wall tiles and some silver picture frames and a comic book with a stranded mermaid on the cover. He found the feira disappointing. An antique shop they came across on their way to the tram struck him however as quite magical. Wooden saints and handcrafted chairs in various states of disrepair and cabinets full of cutlery. He found a pair of crystal shot glasses adorned with filigree ten-pointed stars and thought they would make a fine gift for Marie. The shopkeeper pointed out there was a third glass and he bought all three figuring the third was for Annabelle. Or whomever.

Marco and Gus made their way to a café with a terrace overlooking the rooftops of Alfama. Scaffolds had been raised around some of the buildings and on them shirtless men handled elaborate pulley systems and shouted at one another or parroted the cries of passing seagulls. Marco had a glass of white and smoked half a dozen cigarettes. Gus sipped gingerly from a cup of espresso. They swapped places when the wind changed direction. Gus spoke about Ladino music and its peculiar marriage of Sephardic and Latin traditions. Marco listened without comment and studied his companion's animated and intelligent face. It was a long and narrow face and the effect was heightened by trim black sideburns shot through with wisps of grey. There was a tacit understanding between Marco and Gus that they would probably not meet a third time.

Marco was reminded of his almost friend when he rode the elevador de Santa Justa from Rua do Ouro down to Largo do Carmo. Inside the elevator was a sign that read: Proibido fumar. This had been translated not as Smoking Prohibited or No Smoking but as No Smokers. Marco felt it was taking the matter a bit far.

He had dinner near the Castelho. At the table next to his an elderly couple conversed quietly in the Queen's English. The man spoke at length about his brother's children who he felt were failures or as he said hippies. He attributed this to their having been raised in an overly permissive manner. Marco tried not to listen but couldn't help taking a closer look at the man. A babyfaced giant with rosy cheeks and weak blue eyes. Like someone on a steady diet of pork and antibiotics.

The next day when Marco left the apartment he noticed two cars parked under the orange tree. They looked brand new. Grey and sleek and very clean. He felt they were at odds with the gentle slope of the square and the pastel shades of the buildings. Ambassadors from a world governed by computer assisted design and somehow disturbingly martial.

He walked up the hill. The insistent whir of an electric saw and the clang of metal tools assailed his ears from a nearby construction site. A woman leaned out of a window above him to hang laundry on a clothesline attached to the wall. She dropped her bag of clothes pegs and he tossed it back up. Her face lit up with surprise at her own graceful catch. They smiled and waved at each other before he walked on.

Pneumatic hiss of streetcar brakes. Crackle of sparks on the overhead wire. Weedgrown ledges of the Arco de Cima. Stone walls beleaguered by lichen. Streaks of rust running down a house front from under an iron bar set between windows. A marble doorstep veined with faint strains of grey and lilac. Resonant tolling of distant church bells. A dog yelping in breathless staccato.

On a street corner atop one of the city's many hills he saw a man accompanied by a child. The man said something to a woman standing next to them. The woman gasped and looked where the man was pointing and dropped her bag and raced down the hill. The child grinned delightedly and began to belt after her but was called back by the man. Zacharie, tu restes là. Marco watched for a moment and then proceeded on his way.

He sat for a little while in a café with a handpainted sign on the wall. Cozinha aberta todo o dia. Kitchen never close. Next to the sign was a fuse box and on its lid was a stylised black lightning bolt inside a yellow triangle. Perigo de morte.

Later he watched the sun set above the city's oddly angled rooftops where it left a narrow streak of mauve before this too yielded to the deep blue night. He stepped inside a church on his way back to the apartment and lit candles for his dead under a statue of piousfaced Fatima before concluding the day in his temporary home by drinking a bottle of vinho verde and falling asleep with his shoes and most everything else on.

The next morning he met Ricardo for a late breakfast in a community space on the northern edge of town. They sat at a little table on the sloping concrete floor of what seemed once to have been a garage and ate a dish of scrambled eggs and lettuce. Their plastic cutlery threatened constantly to snap and their paperboard plates to tear. Ricardo spoke about the book he was writing on the history of monetarism in Portugal. Acolytes of the Chicago boys. Takeover first of economics faculties and then of budgetary policy. Role of the central bank. Volume three of Capital. World money.

Mutual friends in Berlin had suggested that Marco meet Ricardo. He reminded Marco of a man Marie and he had shared a kiss with the previous summer at a beachside festival in the province of Oristano on the west coast of Sardinia. Same jet black hair and five-day beard. Same sparkling eyes.

Travelling to the festival had been Marie's idea. An extended weekend of drugs and dancing organised by some friends of hers from Berlin's club scene and a handful of locals who'd raised money at parties to rent a little camping ground off the strada statale. Marie and he had arrived at night in their rented car and pitched their tent at the edge of the macchia and taken some mushrooms and acid and danced all night before going for their first swim in the sea at dawn. They'd meant to arrive a day earlier but had missed their original flight from Tegel following a terrible disagreement over Annabelle that they'd settled by drinking a bottle of Tanqueray. The plane had still been on the tarmac when they'd reached the airport but the lady at the gate had said she couldn't let them board because the system wouldn't allow it. Marco had called her a turgid goblin. The flight they'd eventually caught had involved a layover in Stuttgart and this had caused some apprehension as they'd had to pass through a backscatter x-ray machine at security and had worried about it detecting the condom full of drugs stashed inside Marie's vagina but in fact it had detected nothing and they'd been fine. Their swim in the sea had been marvellous. Everything pristine and crystalline. A world made of light.

Marco remembered all this and the dancing and kissing and all the good conversations as Ricardo told grim tales of sweeping welfare rollbacks and privatisation. They finished their meal and had coffee and smoked a few cigarettes. Ricardo showed Marco the small library he was helping to set up in the community space. Half a dozen shelves stacked with donated books. Mainly but not exclusively political. There were the collected works of Marx and Engels but also some volumes of Joseph Conrad and Hermann Hesse and Jean Chevalier's Dictionary of Symbols.

It's organised thematically, Ricardo explained. He meant the library but Marco's attention was now on the dictionary. He leafed through it starting at the back. He skimmed through the entry on dogs. Something about Samuel Johnson and depression. Butterflies and moths shared an entry. Moths are much older than butterflies, he learned, and they are nocturnal creatures whereas the butterfly is diurnal. Butterflies commence their existence as caterpillars and sustain themselves on nectar. A diet devoid of protein and fat though rich in sugar. The chryscos or cocoon is an image of psychic renewal. In Latin America the butterfly is called mariposa and this is also a colloquial term for whores. Both moths and butterflies are very fragile. See also Animal Life in Nature by Elizabeth Caspari and Animal Spirits by Nicholas Saunders.

Well, Ricardo. This library is a fine idea. Best of luck with it.

Thank you.

They said goodbye. Ricardo returned to the manuscript of a talk he was giving that evening and Marco spent most of the afternoon at the single outdoor table of a bar on Rua Vigario. He drank several glasses of vinho verde and ate a bag of peanuts and looked at the sun and thought about emails he'd received from Annabelle and Marie. Annabelle had sent him a selection of quotations from Pessoa and Marie had written very briefly and simply that she missed him and hoped he was alright. He strolled about a little in the early evening and returned eventually to El Botequim where the same barkeep was on shift. He ignored her scowl and listened with mild annoyance to the monologue a young man with a goatee was delivering to friends or fellow students at the next table. The young man spoke very rapidly as if jacked on speed or thoroughly overcaffeinated. Some poorly considered and redundant argument against what he called the ideology of gender fluidity.

Marco got up late the next day and purchased six euros worth of aspirin from the pharmacy that had sold him the cotton wool for his zippo. By nightfall he felt able to stomach a sandwich and walk down the hill into Bica. He crossed a large square dominated by the floodlit statue of some equestrian national hero. Cars sped by to his right and palm trees rose in silhouette to his left. Beyond the waterfront the Tejo stretched deep black. A small ferry with two decks of brightly lit windows proceeded steadily toward the dim glow of the far bank. The waxing moon was still too slim to properly illuminate the river.

He made his way across Largo de São Paulo shaking his head at offers of cocaine and avoiding the far corner where some ladies of active leisure stood in wait. He pushed through crowds of drinkers and past first-date couples at closely spaced tables. Music from all sides. Fado and samba and plaintive piano tunes. A tall tattooed barkeep poured him a glass of white on Ribeira Nova and he settled onto a folding chair on the sidewalk facing the market hall. Empty stands in the cold fluorescent light of the overhead lamps. Two grey delivery vans parked by the entrance. Clatter of dishes from behind.

When he got up to walk on he was approached again by coke dealers. A man dressed almost entirely in denim seemed especially eager for his custom. Fifty euros for a gram. Heavily cut no doubt. Marco explained he was on a budget and not particularly interested anyhow. Boa sorte, the dealer managed eventually. But not without jerking his chin at a man in a white shirt who was already eyeing Marco from the next corner. Don't buy from him. He is gypsy.

He found a quiet alley and in it a barroom with a door of dark green iron and a window decorated with a faded paper cutting of wine bottles. Two small round tables and a scattering of wooden chairs on a stone floor painted oxblood. He studied the menu chalked onto a blackboard. A thin lady in her late sixties poured him a plastic cup of branco velho. Sweet taste.

He drank the cup and then another two and smoked a few rollups by the door where most of the customers seemed to congregate. Around midnight he decided to make his way back to the apartment. A young woman broke away from the group of friends she'd been talking to and hurried after him. She caught up with him on the corner where the coke dealers were giving an acned backpacker their spiel and planted herself in front of him and fixed her gaze on his. She was slightly out of breath and there was a playfulness in her eyes. Thick strawberry blonde hair falling down past her shoulders and cut crudely into bangs above a face that seemed prone to melancholy but smiled broadly now. She tore a page from the back of a small notebook clad in scuffed black leather and wrote on it and folded it twice and pressed it firmly into his hand. Then she turned around and hurried back to her friends. Marco hesitated for a moment but then walked on. He unfolded the notebook page once he'd left the worst of Bica's nocturnal bustle behind. Written on the page in a blue ballpoint scrawl was a name: Raquel. Beneath the name was a phone number.

When Marco returned to the apartment he found he wasn't very tired. He smoked out the window until the sky began to brighten. Then he lay down on the bed and fell into dreamless slumber. In the morning he brushed his teeth and showered and shaved and went to a nearby bakery to have a coffee and a glass of freshly squeezed orange juice and two pastéis. Later he walked down to the ferry terminal and purchased a return ticket to Cacilhas on the far shore of the Tejo. He sat for half an hour in the waiting room. The vinyl flooring squeaked unpleasantly whenever someone walked on it. Most people around him sat hunched over their mobile phones but everyone looked up when the ferry approached. Mournful grind and creak of the gangway. Straining hawsers. A young man in the ferry company's white uniform hosed down the gangway's creosote surface and the bollards where seagulls had left their greenish grey droppings. Marco found a seat on the upper deck. He felt the thrum of the engine in his feet and buttocks. Names and dates had been scratched into the zinc frame of the window against which he leaned his head. Mario + Zeza. 9-7-83.

Cacilhas was moderately busy on the waterfront with its restaurants and grocery stands but the streets became very quiet within a block or two. Marco found a hairdresser and explained himself by pointing to photographs in magazines. Two ladies with mint green plastic hair rollers all over their heads laughed goodheartedly at this and looked at him with mock concern but he ended up with more or less what he wanted. He strolled about and bought two tangerines for thirty-five cents and sat down on a stone bench to eat them. Across from him was a large building with the words Escola Secundária Gil Vicente above its entrance. Class seemed just to have ended and teenagers walked past him alone and in groups as he tossed the tangerine skins into a wire waste basket beside the bench and wiped his fingers on his chinos. Some of the girls were almost beautiful. Or rather they were but they spoiled it with their awkward gait and the insecurity in their eyes. Marco remembered that difficult age and how uncomfortable he'd felt in his own body. He wished the suffering youngsters well. Everything gets much easier, he wanted to tell them, once you put that fucking escola and its humiliations behind you and lose your virginity and get to drink and smoke legally.

Half an hour later he settled down under the awning of a little café and ordered a salad and a glass of wine. He struck up a conversation with three Dutch ladies in their late fifties and early sixties who were sipping iced soft drinks and sharing a generous serving of fries. The ladies had big arms that were slightly sunburnt and their faces were flushed from the heat. They wore identical sunglasses. Gaudy plastic junk and a little too large.

They knew each other from work. One had just retired and the other two were only a few months away from that felicitous occasion. They asked where Marco was from and he told them.

I was in Berlin last year and found it a terrible town. People there are so impossibly rude.

Ignorant too. I've never met so many ignorant people in any one place.

Marco knew what they meant.

I was riding the bus into Kreuzberg one day. And the bus went by Görlitzer Park. Which isn't really a park at all. More like a big sandpit. It's named after Görlitz. A town in Saxony. I'm sure you know.

Marco nodded.

There was this young man sitting next to me. With his girlfriend. And he was explaining to his girlfriend that the park is named after a Nazi death camp.

Loud groans.

He was thinking of Auschwitz of course. I suppose Görlitz sounds a bit like Auschwitz. But still. Such ignorance.

They talked about Lisbon and exchanged travel tips.

You must go to Belém. It's very pretty.

I think I might.

You smoke a lot, don't you.

Marco braced himself for the usual tiresome lecture.

I like to see people enjoy their cigarettes. Don't listen to all that talk. My husband died of lung cancer. Lifelong nonsmoker. Truth is if that one doesn't get you it'll be some other. Might as well enjoy yourself while you can.

Here's to you.

It was time for Marco to catch the ferry back. He got up and went inside to pay for his meal and came back out and wished the Dutch ladies a pleasant stay. They responded in unison.

Happy days, they said.

Spangles of sunlight on the water. Steady burr of the engine. He watched two seagulls balance on the breeze just aft of the ferry and thought those Dutch ladies were the first people he'd met in Portugal he could imagine himself talking to about Marie and Annabelle and Marie's night at Kit Kat with Julian and how it all made him feel. When he got back to the apartment he saw that Marie and Annabelle had both sent him pictures of themselves. Marie was blowing a kiss at the camera. Annabelle stood on a large stage directing a dozen athletically built dancers. He smoked a few cigarettes out the window and called Raquel. She didn't pick up the phone. He left a message on her answering machine.

The next day he took a train to the beach and wandered for hours past wooden boats turned upside down on the fine white sand. The paint on their hulls blistering. Spume swirled around his ankles and the sun was hot on his shoulders. Occasionally he passed a lone angler seated apathetically on a rock.

He walked a good part of the way back into town and it took him through the parks of Belém where pensioners shuffled about in their Sunday best. Teenagers in swimsuits splashed about in the clear water of a large fountain. The scene made him think of a mass baptism though it was probably just adolescent merriment. Later he walked along a highway with commuters speeding past him on the shimmering blacktop. He reached the towering concrete abutment of the suspension bridge and kept walking. The lanes of the highway were separated by train tracks and on them were stationary freight trains loaded with shipping containers on whose flanks the names of logistics companies and distant ports had been painted. The containers looked abandoned and out of place under the cloudless afternoon sky. Maersk. Hamburg Süd. Hapag Lloyd.

He was back in the city centre by sunset and ate a sandwich before returning to Bica to drink more branco velho in the barroom with the paper cutting of wine bottles in the window. Raquel was nowhere about. A man with a lopsided nose and almost no teeth bummed cigarettes off him and tried to strike up a conversation but the man was so canned he could barely keep from falling over and Marco couldn't make sense of anything he said. The lady behind the bar seemed very patient and gentle with the old swiller. Marco understood why when he considered their features more carefully. They were mother and son. The man confirmed as much when he reached with one hand for Marco's near spent rollup and gestured at the barkeep with the other. Minha mãe, he said. An asinine smile broadened across his face to fully expose the destitute state of his oral cavity. He took the cigarette and shook Marco's hand vigorously before striding with unexpected equipoise across the street where the bouncer outside a small club seemed ready to begin some altercation but then only scowled in grim disapproval. The barkeep's son disappeared around the corner.

A short while later an accordionist swung around the same corner grinning and trying to catch people's eye while squeezing a polka from his poorly tuned instrument. He seemed familiar. Marco made a point of looking the other way but noticed there was a small dog balancing on the accordionist's shoulder. A paper cup in its teeth.

II. Muy Bonito

Something enginepowered was passing when the psilocybin took effect. Perhaps an airplane cutting across the sky. Marco felt restless and slightly nauseous. Then the nausea abated and he began to notice a new crispness to his surroundings as if some original clarity had been restored to his faculties of perception and in particular his vision. All objects perfectly in focus regardless of their proximity or distance.

He looked at the waves and was awed by the generosity of their ceaseless arrival. When he raised his eyes he was struck by the sheer enormity of the open space before and around him. Beyond the scintillating expanse of sea was the bare windsculpted rock of a small island. Mountains rose faintly violet from a stretch of shore behind the island and beyond these mountains was the blue grey intimation of yet another landscape. Horizon after horizon.

There really was a plane in the sky. A tiny shard of gleaming metal receding at the far end of a languidly flaring trail of exhaust fumes. He felt able to reach up and pull down the plane the way he might catch a fly.

The voices of a couple of boys clambering across the rocks on the other side of the bay reached him as clearly as if the two had been standing beside him. His eyes returned to the water that was draped in a quivering web of light. Some large vessel had gone by and the waves heaved and broke more forcefully. The sun was warm on Marco's back. The breeze passed in gentle fluxion around his shoulders. He felt comprehensively caressed.

Marie was sitting next to him now. He turned slowly to look at her. Their gazes locked for a long time and he began to see something in her face that was new to him. A fleshiness and a quality feral and hungry. She must have seen something similar in him because her smile yielded abruptly to a look of distrustful scrutiny. Then they were both smiling again and then laughing with abandon and finally crying.

The waves demanded his attention again. Marie seemed to understand and rose to her feet and tiptoed gingerly over sharp rocks and sat down by herself in a little nook of rosy seawashed granite. Marco breathed deeply and watched the breakers and was unable to come to terms with the wonder of them.

He'd expected the other beachgoers to prove a distraction or even an outright nuisance but they didn't. The young climbers across the bay were not of the landscape but welcome in it. Their talk of how to reach one rock from the other and what could be seen from where would ordinarily have seemed inane to him but he was flush with sympathy now. A group of Spaniards on the beach charmed him by the musical interplay of their vocal timbres. Muy bonito. Muy lindo.

Marie was laughing at a couple that had somehow appeared on the little outcropping of rocks at the centre of the bay. The man stood by while his companion took pictures of herself on her mobile phone. Her long brown hair astir in the breeze. A short while later an elderly man leapt surprisingly from olive foliage and stood with arms outstretched as if to embrace the sea and the sky before vanishing again behind a windblown juniper. There was something magical and mildly comedic about his entry and exit that reminded Marco of a certain painting in the naïve style. Robbers springing upon some unwitting couple in a fairy tale wood. Bauchant, he seemed to remember.

He rejoined Marie. Look at those sailboats. How fast they travel.

Marie nodded.

They're not sailing at all. Their sails are down and their outboards going full throttle.

Some sailors.

Who knows. They may be a long way from port. And they do need to get home on time.

The sun was low already. Soon it began to swell and redden above the trees and the topmost branches and twigs were thrown into filigree silhouette. The air grew chilly. Marco didn't want to leave but he knew the trail leading back to the street was treacherous in the dark.

A group of women emerged from the bottle green macchia and onto the beach where the waves broke at a slight angle and lines of spume raced from the point of first impact to the far edge of the bay like white ribbons unfurling. Now one of the women was in the water and breaststroking from its shallow azure to its deeper emerald regions with her black hair clinging slickly to her head and nape before fraying into a tassel that swayed fluidly and weightlessly about her shoulders and upper back. Marco wanted to feel the water around his own body and Marie nodded encouragingly. The water was cold around his shins and then his knees and then his crotch. He took a deep breath and there was a rushing sound in his ears and his fingers touched the sand that moved in soft sweeping motions and was traversed by slight furrows. He wanted to stay and stay some more but the strain on his lungs proved too much and he steered himself back toward the surface. He took longer to get there than he'd anticipated and for a brief moment he was on the cusp of panic. Then the waves were beneath him again and gently carrying him and he was breathing the evening air.

The moon had risen by the time they ascended the steep and winding trail that had been washed out by heavy rainfall and was bisected in places by the gnarled roots of shrubs and trees. Marie produced an apple from her drawstring bag and offered him a bite.

They reached the hillcrest and the road and rolled cigarettes and smoked. Harsh burn inside his larynx. The sky was a deep blue and the breeze carried odours of broom and mimosa from the dense macchia.

The road took them past a little pizzeria and the sight of people congregating and conversing in the electric light was strangely heartwarming. They reached the house and crouched briefly beside the rosemary bushes to look at the open door next to theirs and the shadows of their neighbours who were seated at the dinner table. The dog picked up their scent and came running excitedly. Marco rubbed the little dip behind its ear.

Marie went to take a shower and Marco sat on the patio outside the kitchen and drank a shot of grappa. It tasted like something that was of a piece with the earth and the trees and even the sky. The stars were out now and there were so many of them. The dog sat by his feet and looked up at him as if he had called to it. He smiled and scratched its neck and then he sat back in his chair and took a deep breath and closed his eyes and said thank you.

III. Nightclubbing

They stood in line outside Kosmonaut treading the pavement and rubbing their hands to dispel the January cold. The bouncer shone a halogen penlight in their eyes. How we doing tonight. It felt all wrong to Marco and he would have turned around and left if it hadn't been for Marie. She knew what to say and when to smile and they were waved through the doorway and even wished a good time by the man in the little wooden stall who took their money and stamped their wrists.

They walked into the narrow courtyard and sat down on a bench fashioned from EPAL pallets and warmed their hands by a mushroom heater and rolled cigarettes and smoked. They could hear the bass from the main floor through a heavy door to their side that was completely covered in stickers advertising club nights and acts. A lady in white hotpants and a silver bomber jacket was doing her makeup above a stainless steel apron sink by the entrance to the bathroom area across from where they were sitting.

Wasn't like this last time I was here, said Marie with a glance at the bouncer. She talked about commercial interests and municipal regulation and about how the club scene was at risk of becoming a parody of what it had been.

The door beside them opened and the bass grew much louder and they could hear people shouting at each other over the music. A sharpfeatured young Arab in a tracksuit stepped into the courtyard. The door fell shut behind him and the noise of the party was muted again. The Arab caught Marie's eye as he walked toward the bathroom area. He passed the lady in the bomber jacket. She had finished doing her makeup and was now filling a small plastic bottle with water from the faucet. The Arab disappeared from sight behind a row of black plywood toilet stalls that were also heavily covered in stickers. Marie had followed his trajectory more attentively than Marco liked but he didn't know what to do about it. I'll be right back, she said and headed to the bathroom area herself.

Marco finished his cigarette and rolled another and lit it. The lady in the bomber jacket smiled briefly at him on her way to the floor. Marco smoked his second cigarette and then a third. When Marie came back she had a sly and gleeful look on her face. She'd removed the brass bobby pins from her rustcoloured curls and touched up her gold eyeliner and her mascara. Let's go, she said and took his hand and led him through the door.

The air inside was heavy with tobacco and weed smoke and humid with perspiration and mingled breath. The music was a pulse in the concrete floor and navigating the space of the room was difficult not just for the push and pull of the crowd but also for the bottles deposited here and there and the broken glass. Bags and jackets on ledges and rafters and on top of speakers. The strobe lights created momentary tableaus of faces and torsos in random constellations and sometimes the afterimage of such a tableau lingered for several seconds in the intervals of darkness.

Marco was by himself for lengths of time as Marie explored the other floors. A young man in military pants and a tank top and a baseball cap approached him and shouted something about a team and waited for a response and then shouted something else until Marco understood he was also by himself and looking for a wing man. Marco smiled and shook his head. When Marie came back they had vodka shots at the bar and then she took his hand again and showed him around the other floors and told him she didn't much like the crowd or the music. They ended up kissing and making out on a faux leather sofa. The man in military pants walked by and gave Marco the thumbs up.

They didn't dance very much that night. Just consider it an extended walk, said Marie after a few hours and they returned to the poorly lit street with its crunching gravel and patches of dirty snow. The light in the subway station seemed almost painfully glaring. Marie fell asleep two stops from home with her temple resting against Marco's collarbone and her breathing in time with the motion of his fingers in her hair.

Their next outing was to Griessmühle on the industrial perimeter of Neukölln. A former factory between a scrapyard and the canal. The main floor was a concrete pit overlooked by steel balconies and the dancers were a throbbing cluster of bodies intermittently illuminated by the ice blue flash of lamps bolted in geometric patterns to iron rafters. People tore up paperboard flyers and rolled them into little tubes and used them to snort lines of speed and ketamine and cocaine off the displays of their mobile phones in the cramped upstairs bathroom area and a lady was fucking loudly in one of the stalls.

The chillout area was simply the muddy bank of the canal with its view of two container cranes and a wall topped with razor wire. Someone had built a fire and a small group of people in hoodies sat around it smoking quietly. Marco was led there by Marie around six in the morning. She'd found him stooped and dry retching between a speaker and a stack of beer crates on one of the smaller floors and now he was shirtless and bigeyed and in a cold sweat.

So maybe natura non facit, he spat. But these pills certainly do.

What happened?

I don't know. Everything was fine until the set ended and the lights came on. It was so sudden. Everyone just left and the light was brutal. Like a fucking scalpel to the eye.

She handed him her water bottle and he drank from it at length. The water was very cold but it cleared his head.

Where were you anyway?

I met some friends. But I was keeping you in sight the whole time.

Pills didn't do a thing for me all night. I was just wondering where you'd gone and whether you'd come back. Then I thought I saw someone I know. Then the music ended and the lights came on and everyone left and my feet soared up and hit the ceiling over and over and I wanted to vomit but couldn't and my clothes were completely soaked from one moment to the next and it just felt like my body was trying to turn itself inside out.

Marie handed him his shirt and his sweater and he pulled them on and finished the water and smoked cigarette after cigarette until his heartbeat slowed and his chest stopped heaving. The fire was dying down and the other people had left except for a finelimbed man in his twenties who sat staring at the embers where they flared white and gold in the breeze. He looked very tired. When he asked for a cigarette and Marie rolled him one he smiled and his smile seemed like that of an old man as interpreted by a young man's features. He said he hadn't slept in three days and Marie nodded to signal her familiarity with that territory.

They sat in silence for a time. Then Marco and Marie got to their feet and wished the young man well and returned inside to continue dancing. By the time the sun was up they were sharing the last open floor with only two other people. It was the smallest floor and the multicoloured pennant banner and the decorations of tinted paper and rainbow foil that had been attached to the ceiling and the walls looked tawdry in the cold daylight seeping past the edges of steel window shutters. Men were hauling beer crates back and forth by the bar and someone was restocking the tall black refrigerator. The ground was littered with dog ends and crushed paper cups and torn flyers and the little polyethylene ziplock bags that drugs were traded in. The music ended around noon. Marco and Marie donned their sunglasses and popped gum into their mouths and said goodbye to the bouncers and walked home along the canal. Its perfectly still surface mirrored with striking exactitude the brick warehouses and the billboards and trees and even the secondary reflection of all this in their sunglass lenses.

Marco felt he was getting the knack of things by their third outing. He'd learned to stay away from certain pills and stick to mushrooms and acid and weed and maybe some molly. He was offered a line of cocaine when he helped a distraught man in an oversized white puff jacket locate a lost mobile phone. He sat talking with Marie and when the crowd had thinned somewhat they danced for seven or eight hours. At one point Marie led him to the bathroom area and took him inside one of the stalls and bolted the door and squatted before him and unbuckled his belt and unbuttoned his fly and pulled his cock from his boxers and put it in her mouth. They fucked extensively and then freshened up by the sink and had a couple of vodka shots at the bar before dancing for several hours more and repeating the operation. By early afternoon they were in his apartment. He fixed them some scrambled eggs and they opened a bottle of red and ate the eggs very slowly and drank the red and smoked a few joints and had sex again before falling asleep in each other's arms feeling warm and thoroughly spent. Two children were loudly racing their tricycles across the yard and shouting and the upstairs neighbour was strumming his guitar and these sounds insinuated themselves into Marco's and Marie's sleep but did not wake them.

IV. Mezcal

Hecho en Oaxaca, Mexico. The agave spirit made for strange dreams. Marco found out the night he and Marie elected a bottle of San Cosme as an addition to their usual small hour routine of talking and making love and decimating the day's purchase of rolling tobacco. The first light of dawn was seeping through the burgundy curtains and falling on the fluid organic patterns traced by the grain of the old pinewood floorboards when he woke breathless and primed for violent action by surging adrenalin. He was sweating heavily and his heartbeat was frenzied. These observations and the thoughts that flowed from them and then spun themselves on by the familiar concatenating action of his intellect seemed to him to be borne by something more primordial that was to the mind like the churning of a vast black ocean to the evanescent play of spume on wavecrests and had in some obscure sense been the subject of the dream he'd woken from. He tried to recall the dream's events but succeeded only partially and the prime impression remained that of this force that appeared to be endowed with its own volition and struck him as deeply and disturbingly hostile. Marie and he had been engaged in a contest whose rules had demanded that one of them destroy the other. They'd worked with frightening purpose and cruel lucidity to bring each other death and had he not awoken he would have become either killer or kill. Not as in an altercation whose consequence its protagonists fail to foresee but by an act thoroughly premeditated and perversely artful.

Marie told him her dream when she woke up a little later. She'd been on a bus with him or perhaps a train. It had been a very large vehicle because they'd lost one another and she'd taken a long time to find him again. She'd searched dimly lit aisles and cramped compartments and had apologized to strangers and shrugged off expressions of annoyance as she'd moved further and further down what had eventually presented itself as a steel tunnel designed to steadily erode her confidence in herself and her surroundings and the friend she'd been seeking. She'd finally found him in the arms of two women and he'd spoken animatedly and at length about himself and his virtues. He hadn't paid much attention to her. In fact he hadn't seemed to know her at all. She'd woken with a sense of paralysis. As unable to leave as to stay.

V. Kit Kat

They're not letting anyone through except guys in latex, said the man in the shortsleeved floral print shirt as he returned from the door and strode back past the queue. Marco and Marie and Julian stood smoking and patiently waiting their own turn to be scrutinised by the stocky bouncers. They were also waiting for Julie to return from the late night store with the beer she'd been craving. Two thinly dressed and heavily tattooed American ladies behind them spent most of their wait discussing food. Burger this and burger that. The man in the white suit just in front of them overheard Marie talking about the pool and threatened with a wink to push her in later.

That they'd even made it this far seemed a feat. Marie had badly cut her finger in the kitchen as she was prone to doing when excited. Julian's Turkish guest Gaye had joined them for a dinner of soup and had for once not thought out loud about whether catching her return flight to Istanbul was a good idea in light of the Turkish president's increasingly authoritarian antics. Journalists arrested for mentioning the Armenian genocide and so forth. That evening she'd been in shock and in tears because her pet dog Luca had been bitten to death by some local beast four times its size. Of all the fucked up experiences awaiting unsuspecting visitors to Berlin.

Julie was back with her beer now and smiling that smile of hers that always looked a little sad. She drank the beer and placed the empty bottle on the curb and they smoked more cigarettes and then they were at the front of the queue.

You must be on the guest list, said the brawniest of the bouncers with a grin. Presumably in reference to Marie. Emerald teddy and matching lipstick. Though Julian's crocodile leather vest was not so bad either. All Marco and Julie had to show was the fading ink of a few tattooed skulls and serpents and vampire bats.

No GHB, read the sign taped to the door. Behind the door was a petite young lady with short black hair and a light silver chain linking her nose and ear piercings. All she wore. She had trouble scanning one of their tickets and held the scanner to the QR code three different ways before giving up and waving them on to the coat check. They handed over their mobile phones. No discussion. We've had too much hassle with people taking pictures.

Marco got vodka shots as the others settled down by the pool. The barkeep was also in her birthday suit and got a lot of stares from her male customers. Push and pull of the crowd. Orders shouted or mouthed with multiple fingers raised and bills and change reached over people's shoulders and heads.

Julian and Julie had disappeared somewhere when Marco returned to the pool. Fast bunch. Marie and he drank the four shots and watched the lady on the swing above the water. Half a dozen people got up from the far side of the pool to congregate around an arched doorway painted lime green beyond which a larger cluster of onlookers stood cheering. Marco and Marie couldn't see what was prompting the cheers but they could guess.

They got up eventually and headed for the dance floor. They passed a white vinyl sofa on which a man in a studded leather mask lay flaunting his erection as others stood about smoking impassively. On a little balcony above the dance floor was an old steel gynecology chair on which two heavyset men were having sex. A young man with the broad shoulders and slim waist of a competitive swimmer stood bent over a speaker. He pulled his pink speedos down past his buttocks and held up three fingers and was lashed three times with a horsewhip before pulling his speedos back up and nodding thanks.

There was another swing by the deejay booth. Marie sat down on it to sway gently and smoke as Marco danced. A woman to his side reminded him of Annabelle. She was blonde and nude except for the canvas pouch strapped to her thigh and the black bandana covering her face below the eyes. He glanced in Marie's direction and noticed a man with long brown curls relighting her cigarette and talking to her. Marco walked over and joined Marie on the swing. The man took off.

A woman with a buzzcut and a slew of facial piercings stepped into the room and strutted along the edge of the dance floor with her boyfriend behind her on a leash. Marco raised one foot onto the swing and reached inside his shoe to retrieve a small bag containing five grams of methylenedioxymethamphetamine. Not those weak grey crystals sold in the park but quality stuff. Like refined sugar. Marie administered. She wet her pinky and dipped it in the bag and then between Marco's lips before repeating the procedure for herself. They washed down the bitter chemical taste with a few mouthfuls of water from her bottle and kissed.

The deejay was ending his set and the floor was being closed as they were coming up. They got off the swing and headed next door. Someone had left a thin leather belt on a speaker and Marco picked it up and hung it around Marie's neck.

At the far end of the next floor was a low pedestal with a chrome dance pole fixed between it and the ceiling. Marie stepped onto the pedestal and wrapped herself around the pole and twisted lithely. Marco danced beside her and they were soon joined by a man in his sixties whose body was an elaborate picture book of old tattoos. Bold black lines fading into green. A coiled serpent on his gut and a swooping eagle above it. An ace of spades and a sailor's grave across his ribs. Schooner sinking inside a bottle. Also a lady sitting in a cocktail glass. Man's ruin.

There were little platforms and balconies around and above the dance floor where people were having sex in groups of three or four. Sometimes just a single couple with others standing or sitting nearby and watching.

Julian and Julie were dancing near the bar and Marco approached them to see how they were doing. Julian said he'd overdone the molly and thrown up but was feeling better now. He was gurning badly. Marco got a stick of chewing gum from Marie and gave it to him.

Later Marco and Marie set off to explore the further reaches of the club. The place really was a labyrinth. Always another floor. Doors sometimes open and sometimes locked. An extensive basement with stairs and corridors leading to small rooms or nowhere at all. Three women dressed as nurses leaning over a hospital bed. I think we've lost him, said one in a tone of mock distress and the others giggled. Taped to the brick wall was an anatomical chart. At the bottom of the chart were simple black and white drawings illustrating pelvic floor exercises.

They descended another flight of stairs and stooped to pass through a low doorway. Beyond it was a small strobelit dance floor with perhaps a dozen dancers and beyond the dance floor were more white vinyl sofas. Marco and Marie settled down beside a sleeping man dressed only in sneakers and talked. Marco told Marie he loved her more than he'd ever loved anyone and she kissed him and then she unbuttoned his jeans. They'd been fucking for a good twenty minutes when the set ended and the lights came on. The crowd cheered and clapped. Marco extricated himself from between Marie's legs and she slipped the crotch of her teddy back into place and he buttoned his fly and they both laughed. The dancers dispersed with much hugging and kissing. Someone handed the deejay a joint and he accepted it with a nod and a gracious smile. A man in dungarees began sweeping the room. He avoided the sofa area for a time but eventually he approached Marco and Marie and politely threw them out. The man who'd been sleeping beside them was gone. They rejoined Julian and Julie by the pool. People sat talking or touching up their lipstick. Most wore shades to soften the sunbeams that fell through a skylight.

The streets were deserted except for an occasional group of party people and sometimes a pensioner. They walked into Kreuzberg past used car dealers and gas stations and the spraypainted concrete façades of housing projects. They paused for half an hour by the canal to sit on a low stone wall and smoke cigarettes and look at the sun on the water. Later they smoked a gram of weed on Julian's cluttered balcony and killed a bottle of red wine and washed it down with several large glasses of gin and orange juice each. Best cure for alcoholism, said Marco. A quip he remembered from Lowry. Julian fetched his mobile phone and they recorded a voice message for poor Gaye. They drew together in a close embrace before withdrawing to their beds with bottles and tobacco pouches in hand.

VI. The Movie

It's an idiom from the French, Marco explained. L'embarras des richesses. An overabundance.

But why embarrassment?

I suppose it could be embarrassing to live in overabundance when others have little or even nothing.

This is why you're frowning?

No. My head.

Marie kissed him tenderly on the temple and got out of bed and went into the kitchen. She returned with a glass of tap water and dropped an aspirin into it. Marco thanked her and waited for the aspirin to dissolve and drank the water. The last sip tasted chalky.

Maybe if someone had more going on than they could handle they would find that embarrassing.

Do you have more going on than you can handle?

I didn't say that.

Marie began to count on her fingers. Annabelle. Monica. Mara and Christian. Mo. The one who left with that belt you gave me. What was her name?

We never found out.

Marco rolled a cigarette and lit it. I'm feeling very doted upon and I'm grateful is all I meant.

How do you feel about breakfast?

He finished his cigarette and got up and went into the kitchen and filled the hopper of the old oakwood coffee mill with coffee beans and pressed the mill firmly down against the table and spun the iron lever until the hopper was empty. He poured hot water into a Neapolitan flip coffee pot and spooned the ground coffee from the drawer at the base of the mill into the basket and screwed on the perforated lid and fit the collector on top and set the coffee pot on the stove. He heated some olive oil in a stainless steel porringer and tossed in some dried chili and two cloves of garlic and broke six eggs. He scrambled the eggs and added some cherry tomatoes and a slice of ham and a pinch of salt and a generous amount of black pepper. The napoletana had begun to hiss and blow steam from its spout and he removed it from the stove and turned it around to let the coffee run through. He scraped the contents of the porringer into two small ceramic bowls and stuck a fork in each and placed the bowls on a round brass tray along with the coffee pot and two tin cups and carried the tray to the bed. He glanced at the little clock on his desk along the way and saw that it was ten in the evening.

Later they snorted some ketamine off the pocket mirror by the bedside and waited for the odd sense of weightlessness. Like getting your legs kicked out from under you but never falling. They fucked for several hours and mostly he couldn't tell which part of his body was touching which part of hers or what it meant or whether it mattered. Even their orgasms became indistinguishable. Sometimes it seemed as if the entire room were climaxing.

They shared some 2C-B the next night. Marie put the pink pill between her teeth and bit it in half along the cleft. They washed the two halves of the pill down with water and soon a metallic taste and a gentle tugging sensation along the gums alerted them they were coming up. For six hours their surroundings were basked in soft mauve and violet tones and there was a slight sparkle to each object. They felt deeply at peace. It's as if time were standing still or didn't exist at all or were somehow dissolved in this motion, said Marie. This motion that everything is swept up in.

They got up around nightfall the following day and smoked a joint in the bathtub and listened to Chet Baker sing Blue Moon and My Foolish Heart. Marco cooked tortiglioni with diced aubergines and goat cheese and a few leaves of sage. They ate their meal at the kitchen table in the light of three candles and a fanous suspended from the doorjamb. The glass of the fanous was tinted burgundy and bottle green and ultramarine and amber. They drank a litre of wine and smoked another joint and listened to more records before returning to bed and dropping some acid. The tabs were from a batch Marie had bought from her Kreuzberg dealer and Marco always responded very strongly to them. That night he looked at Marie lying beneath him and saw her face transform into someone else's and then someone else's again. This continued for several minutes. Certain faces he recognised and others he had never seen before though they seemed equally real. One of the faces was Marie's but she was much younger. They took more of the same acid another night and the band-aid on Marie's finger slipped off as they were fucking. Soon Marie's stomach and breasts were smeared with blood and Marco had a frenzied vision of himself cutting and stabbing both of them with a knife. Sometimes he felt there was someone else in the room and once he spoke words to Marie that he was certain were not his own.

They began to run out of drugs as well as money after a few

weeks. It was the end of the month and the balance of Marco's bank account was too low to cover the rent. Marie arranged to meet an aunt she was sometimes able to borrow money from. Marco kissed her goodbye at the door and watched her skip down the stairs. Then he went into the bathroom and brushed his teeth and took a long hot shower. He combed his hair and wet a handful of baking soda and rubbed it under his armpits. He filled a teacup with hot water and placed his shaving brush inside. He took his straight razor from its black leather case and pulled the cowhide strop hanging from the brass door handle taut and passed the razor over the strop fifty times. Then he unscrewed the lid from a tin of shaving soap and worked up a good lather with the brush and applied the soap to his face. He shaved closely against and across the grain. He rinsed the brush and held the razor in cold water for half a minute before drying it carefully and placing it back in its leather case. He dabbed his face with a towel and smeared some petroleum jelly on his chin where he'd opened a little cut from a previous shave. Then he went into the bedroom and put on a fresh pair of boxers and some socks and stepped into his jeans and buttoned the fly and buckled the belt. He pulled on a clean shirt and a denim jacket and slipped on his shoes and tied the laces. He put his keys in the front pocket of his jeans and his billfold in the back pocket and took a drawstring bag from the nail hook by the door and walked over to the bookshelf and stashed half a dozen clothbound volumes in the bag and slung it over his shoulder and left the apartment to take the subway to Kottbusser Tor.

Marco arrived just within the bookstore's opening hours and browsed the shelves while Patrick researched the market value of Rosa Luxemburg's collected works on the computer.

Volumes six and seven?

Weren't published until ten years later. This is all I have.

Patrick sat chewing his underlip. I can give you thirty euros.

Marco signed the receipt and took the three bills and slipped them into his billfold.

Thanks for helping me out.

My pleasure as always.

Marco stepped outside and into a slight drizzle. He walked to the bank and deposited the money and headed toward the subway station. He felt someone was following him and turned around to look. A rangy man in a grey coat. Homeless judging by the state of his beard and the grime on his face. Clear blue eyes. A piercing gaze.

The man asked for a cigarette and Marco rolled him one. Opening his jacket and hunching forward slightly to keep the paper from getting wet.

What's that scar on your forehead?

Marco looked at the man. There's no scar on my forehead.

No. What they said to me.

There was no scar on the other's forehead either as far as Marco could tell. He handed the man his cigarette and lit it.

I told them I fell over. None of their business.

That's right. Marco had resumed walking toward the subway station. The man walked beside him.

What are you doing harassing these women?

I'm sorry?

What they said. They were going to sue me for molestation.

That so.

I've got my wits about me, you know. I told them: You sue me for molestation and I'll sue you for denial of assistance.

They'd reached the yellowtiled entrance to the station. Look brother, I've got a train to catch.

The man drew on his cigarette and fixed his clear blue eyes on Marco and said: You be on your way now. I'll see you in the movie.

VII. Closing

Brussels airport was state of the art. Sterile effulgence. A complex of glass passages designed to promote high technology and other investment opportunities to supermen in transit. Advertisements looming above the moving walkway. No object depicted there that wasn't sleek and almost weightless. No human figure that wasn't pale and ethereal. Ambassadors of a luminous silver world made of money and information and power. We never eat. We only glow. Passengers for Swiss three-four-five-nine, please make your way to gate sixty-four. We are now closing the gate.

Duty free. Cornucopia of chocolates and perfumes and liquor and cigarettes. Marco looked for a carton of filterless Luckies but there was none. The whiskey section was more or less up to scratch though nothing to write home about. In Marco's unenlightened opinion. A real superman would no doubt have bought it all. The chocolates and the perfumes and the liquor and the cigarettes. Gifts for the wife or the affair or tomorrow's business partner. The larger shopping area beyond the duty free zone would have seen said superman continue his spree by purchasing socks and underwear and sneakers and baseball caps and brogues and dinner jackets. Perhaps a car. There were several parked on low platforms. Black and space grey and very polished.

Then the treadmills. Plastic contraptions bolted to the floor in two rows of eight for the unwillingly and unacceptably sedentary flier to exercise on. All energy generated by the consummation of your long frustrated desire for physical activity will be fed directly into your mobile phone. Ward off that heart attack while checking emails.

Fashion stores. Partake of Victoria's secret. All major credit cards accepted. Young saleswoman between clothes racks. Same black outfit. Subdued lighting. No one else in the shop. The potential customers were outside. Transfixed by a wall of television screens. Model strutting in jewelled negligé. Neither mermaid nor amazon. She had legs and Marco counted two breasts. Though she was hardly human either. In fact she had wings. Two perfectly symmetric cascades of iridescent sequins.

Food court. Marco was hungry but nothing was affordable. He could have taken both Marie and Annabelle out to dinner for what would here have bought him a slice of cheese on a shabby excuse for white bread. A cigarette at least? The lounge one floor above looked promising. But he was gently informed that his kind was unwelcome. You needed a rich man's ticket to get past the glass door. There was something advertising itself as a sports bar. It closed at seven. A tiredfaced Moroccan had just finished wiping the chrome counter and locking away the drinks when Marco arrived.

What about that smoking area? It had been closed on his way to Lisbon. I'm sorry, sir. Our smoking area doesn't open until two. It was open now but they sure did a good job of hiding the place. Very end of the walkway. You needed a fair amount of time and a certain resolve to get there. A filthy little trash can of a room where the terminal terminated. Step inside and see what we think of you. Space for three people. Ashtrays not emptied for days. Dog ends all over the floor. An electric fan whirring busily in the corner. There might as well have been a sign by the entrance: Smoke if you must but don't expect us to clean up after you. We want the angels to ourselves and our boss said we may just get inside their panties if we always check those emails on time.

I guess this is the future, Marco muttered. He couldn't stand it.

VIII. Opening

Marco pulled the old door shut behind him and crossed the little square and descended the steps to Largo de São Paulo. He passed the Cais do Sodré and walked along the waterfront on Avenida 24 de Julho before turning right toward the dimly lit alleys of Bica. Usual bustle of nighthawks. Clusters of smokers outside bars. A young couple peering down from a stone arch bridge. Four nervous bouncers by the entrance to a strip joint. And of course the eagereyed dealers. Jealously guarding their territories and ever on the lookout for custom.

He found Raquel at the far end of a hardwood plank veranda behind one of the more well concealed bars. She was sitting at a little iron bistro table with a glass of white and a book and an ashtray. Same look of settled sadness. Though he could see fresh brushstrokes being applied to that grounding as he approached. A sudden sparkle in her eye. A charming smile.

You kept me waiting.

Not too long, I hope.

He sat down across from her and they ordered more wine and

smoked and talked about José Maria Branco and Frank O'Hara and Julio Cortázar and Carol Dunlop and Richard Hell. They talked about aborted relationships and loss and the ways one fools oneself and others. Marco put his hand on hers and then on her knees and they kissed. They talked about rent hikes and the gentrification of Lisbon and the legacy of the Salazar regime and the price and quality of Bica cocaine. They kissed again and debated with ritualised incertitude the question of whether to climb the hill to his room and fuck or just call it a night.

The walk seemed longer than usual. They passed a dark church and several miradouros where tourists stood taking pictures of the Castelho and the slope of the Bairro Alto. The alleys around the apartment were deserted and quiet except for the sound of traffic from downtown. The apartment seemed small and cramped. Marco steered Raquel toward the bed and gently pushed her onto it and pulled off her shoes and socks. He lay down beside her and she pressed herself against him. She raised her arms above her head and he pulled off her top and then her bra. He put one breast in his mouth and then the other. He passed his tongue over the sides and undersides of her breasts and then over her ribs and her navel and the soft little mound below. He pulled off her pants and her panties and licked the inside of her thighs. She put her hands around the back of his head. His tongue moved inside her until she shuddered. The alarm clock ticking on the nightstand briefly reminded him of the flight he was catching in the morning but he put this out of his mind. They screwed for several hours and it ended with a general sense of disequilibrium. As if the world were tipping and everything about to fall and maybe break. Through the half open window came the sound of a dog barking frantically in response to their cries.

They lay for a long time on the tangled sheets before rising to stand by the window and smoke. There was a freighter on the river and the steady rotation of its radar in the early light appeared from where they stood like a slow switching motion.

John

John placed his large hands flat on the tabletop as if to hold it in place. He looked down at the cooling cup of black before him so that his eyes were barely visible under his eyelids as he spoke. What I remember most clearly about my drinking days is a persistent sense of shame. You notice a certain consternation in people. They seldom do a good job of concealing the discomfort you provoke in them. You also know fairly certainly that you're being gossiped about. More than others, I mean. What's in some ways worse insofar as it's not a matter of human cruelty but has the makings of the supernatural and often positively of witchcraft is the damned proneness to accidents. Objects seemed to always be breaking or malfunctioning when I drew near. Often in ways that defied rational explanation. I can't tell you how many times I nearly burned down the house. I suppose handling open fire and negotiating city traffic are already associated with a certain degree of apprehension in the mind of any sane person. I began to think of them as forms of Russian roulette. As near suicidal undertakings or feats you may accomplish once but had better not attempt routinely. This lasted weeks into my dry spells. It was often worst before the day's first drink. So it wasn't what our legislators had in mind when they decreed we shouldn't drive under the influence.

You can talk about it in terms of clumsiness and distraction if you like but said clumsiness and distraction were less a consequence of acute intoxication than a constant condition. It's something that creeps up on every steady drinker and then stays. It's there with them regardless of whether they happen at any particular moment to be tight or not. Your nerves are shot all the time. But don't get me wrong. I'm not talking about the shakes. I didn't even have those the first few years and yet I was always dropping things or slipping or tripping and near breaking my neck. Not just in unfamiliar alleys but in my own bedroom and kitchen. Some sort of chronic ineptness. Though mostly it didn't seem as if I was to blame so much as my surroundings. As if the trappings of everyday life had somehow conspired against me. That was the worst part. Much worse than the shame and worse than the amply documented health issues. The nausea and the headaches and the feeling your guts have been in an acid bath. The rotten taste every forenoon. Like you've slept with a leather glove in your mouth, Chandler says somewhere. Or maybe he says motorman's glove. I don't remember. Leather would be underplaying it insofar as that word suggests some more or less artful treatment of animal matter whereas to me the taste was always brutally that of the unhandled carcass. Then of course there's the sheer feebleness. You're simply and perennially sick and drained. Your physical substance worn thin from forever sailing against the wind. The slightest shove will send you toppling. Like glasses stacked with the idiotic optimism of the inebriate to some thoroughly unreasonable height. Courting disaster. Your knees are always trembling too. It's not just the hands. Of course you always talk yourself into believing the next potation will remedy it all. Putting out the fire with gasoline, as they say. But forget all that. The worst part of the whole sordid business is the suspicion and later the certainty that you've been judged irredeemably corrupt and hence expelled not just from the community of respectable men but even from the larger physical world. People talk about being out of it or floating in space but that's just bad poetry. Doesn't even come close. Hell, it's like the whole fucking universe turns its back on you.

Water to the Drowned

Someone had left the water running. Mackerel bones and garlic skins spun languidly around the steel sink strainer. There was a dark wine stain on the rug and salt had been strewn over it. On the table were stacks of unwashed dinner plates and a brass ashtray overflowing with the dog ends of rollups and machinofactured filter cigarettes. Lipstick traces on some of the latter. Next to the ashtray were six shot glasses stacked one inside the other to form a precariously leaning tower that called to mind the signature architectural mishap of a certain Tuscan town. Or the bard:

> Like a drunken sailor on a mast,
> Ready with every nod to tumble down
> Into the fatal bowels of the deep.

Now the phone was ringing. A series of shrill peals as offensive to the ear as the afternoon sun was to the eye. He had no intention of answering. He found a bottle with enough gin left in it to burn the rotten taste off his tongue but his tobacco was nowhere to be found. Even the spare pack he kept in the drawer with the matches and candles and lighter fluid was gone. He searched the drawer more thoroughly but the result was the same. No tobacco.

The phone fell silent in mid peal. No better music than silence. Who said that? Don't remember. He cleared a space on the table for the oakwood coffee mill and filled the hopper and spun the lever. He found and assembled the four components of his napoletana and set it on the crusted stove. There was a knock on the door. It gave him a jolt. He thought for a moment he'd misheard but when the knock was repeated he realised he hadn't. Someone in the stairway wanted a word. He chose to ignore.

The small refrigerator in the corner began to hum and shudder and the empty lager bottles deposited on top of it stirred in faint tintinnabulation. The knocking ceased. Often pays to wait things out, he thought. Just then the upstairs neighbour began drilling. Or perhaps the downstairs neighbour. Hard to tell sometimes in these old buildings. Bronze bells commenced to clamour solemnly in the church tower across the street. Three chimes meant three o'clock. Or three quarters to the hour. Or that a burial was being concluded.

He found an apple in the red wire hanging basket and sat down on the screwtop stool by the window and ate the apple while waiting for steam to blow from the spout of the napoletana. The knocking resumed. He placed the apple core on the tea tin that shared the windowsill with a bowl of eggs and another of tomatoes and a stunted San Pedro cactus in a terracotta flower pot. He went into the bathroom and took his kimono from the nail hook by the mirror and slipped it on and tied the sash. It was a children's kimono and only reached halfway to his knees but he liked its filigree blue and white dragon motif. He walked to the front door and opened the lock and lowered the handle and took a step back as he pulled the door toward him.

Marie's blue eyes peered serenely and curiously at him from her faintly freckled face. Rusty tousle of her ungovernable curls. Rainbow-coloured earrings he'd brought back from Buenos Aires years ago. Short black summer dress embroidered in gold and vermilion. Fishnet stockings. A bottle in her tote bag and a large amaryllis in her right hand. She said: I wanted to see you. It's been too long. And I'd like a drink. Perhaps you'll have it with me. He remembered reading somewhere about the association of beauty with the unexpected but he couldn't recall the exact argument and it seemed a bit lofty anyhow. Come in, he said more simply. I'll rinse two glasses and you can tell me where you've been all this time. She stepped inside and he shut the door behind her. An afterthought asserted itself. You wouldn't have a smoke by any chance?

Berlin, 2016–2023